VIRAGO
MODERN CLASSICS
632

P. L. Travers was born Helen Lyndon Goff in 1899 in Queensland, Australia. She worked as a dancer and an actress, but writing was her real love and she turned to journalism. Travers set sail for England in 1924 and became an essayist, theatre and film critic, and scholar of folklore and myth. While recuperating from a serious illness Travers wrote *Mary Poppins* – 'to while away the days, but also to put down something that had been in my mind for a long time,' she said. It was first published in 1934 and was an instant success. *Mary Poppins* has gone on to become one of the best-loved classics in children's literature and has enchanted generations. In addition to the *Mary Poppins* books, Travers wrote novels, poetry and non-fiction. She received an OBE in 1977 and died in 1996.

By P. L. Travers

Aunt Sass: Christmas Stories

I Go by Sea, I Go by Land

The Fox at the Manger

Friend Monkey

Mary Poppins

Mary Poppins Comes Back

Mary Poppins Opens the Door

Mary Poppins in the Park

Mary Poppins in Cherry Tree Lane

Mary Poppins in the House Next Door

I GO BY SEA,
I GO BY LAND

P. L. Travers

With drawings by Gertrude Hermes

virago

VIRAGO

This edition published in Great Britain in 2015 by Virago
First published in Great Britain in 1941 by Peter Davies Limited

1 3 5 7 9 10 8 6 4 2

Copyright © Trustees of the P. L. Travers Will Trust, 1941

The moral right of the author has been asserted.

A CIP catalogue record for this book
is available from the British Library.

ISBN 978-0-349-00574-4

Typeset in Fournier by M Rules
Printed and bound in Great Britain by
Clays Ltd, St Ives plc

Papers used by Virago are from well-managed forests
and other responsible sources.

MIX
Paper from
responsible sources
FSC® C104740
www.fsc.org

Virago Press
An imprint of
Little, Brown Book Group
100 Victoria Embankment
London EC4Y 0DY

An Hachette UK Company
www.hachette.co.uk

www.virago.co.uk

Matthew, Mark, Luke and John,
Bless the bed that I lie on.
Before I lay me down to sleep
I give my soul to Christ to keep.
Four corners to my bed,
Four angels round me spread,
Two to foot and two to head
And four to carry me when I'm dead.
I go by sea, I go by land,
The Lord made me with His right hand.
If any danger come to me,
Sweet Jesus Christ deliver me.
He is the branch and I am the flower,
Pray God send me a happy hour,
And if I die before I wake
I pray that Christ my soul will take.

TO MICHAEL SHANNON

THIS STORY OF A VOYAGE WITH LOVE

The characters in Sabrina's diary and the experiences recorded are authentic. It is a personal record and certain names have necessarily been altered. Also, in view of present conditions in Great Britain it seemed wiser to suppress specific dates and any mention of ports of sailing, and to hide under the pseudonym of Thornfield the true identity of the village from which this journey started.

P. L. T.

ILLUSTRATIONS

PART I

'I GO BY SEA'

Now I am going to write a Diary because we are going to America because of the War. It has just been decided. I will write down everything about it because we shall be so much older when we come back that I will never remember it if I do not. So this is the beginning.

I am Sabrina Lind, eleven years and three months and my Brother is James Lind aged nearly Nine. We are going to America because of the War. At first they thought it would be all right to let us stay at home in Sussex and just have lessons with Miss Minnett and Mr Oliphant as we did when we were Young. When we grew out of Miss Minnett she stayed on to do the mending and housekeeping and generally Potter. Miss Minnett is Fifty-two and has a Bed-ridden sister. Mr Oliphant is the Vicar of Thornfield and nobody knows how old he is. He was the one who used to teach James Latin and Mathematics and me Birds and their Nests about which he knows a good deal.

Father said that our house which is called Thornfield (just like the Village) had stood for over nine hundred years and was old enough to take care of itself and would probably go on standing no matter what happened. Also, that as there was nothing round it but fields and farms nobody would want to drop bombs on it as it wasn't a Military Object. He and Mother kept on saying that but James and I could see that they were nervous so we kept very quiet and stayed out of their way so that they should not notice us much. But all through the summer they seemed to notice us more than ever and we had special Treats like using up the last of the petrol to go to the Sea and killing off Mrs Metcalfe and Mrs de Quincy, two special hens, to supplement the meat Ration. Also more than the usual number of picnics. And each time we did these things it seemed to be the last time, as though we were saying goodbye to everything every minute. We were not the only ones, because Jason and Jane and Mirabel Campbell and Robert and Anna Eridge and Matthew Scott, our childhood Freinds, came to stay with us so that they could be safely out of London. And all of us felt the same thing, that this summer was not like all the other summers but only a Farewell.

And it turned out to be just that because very soon Jason and Jane and Mirabel and Robert and Anna went to America and Matthew was sent to a Boarding-school in the West Country so as to be as far from the East as possible because his Father, who is a man of Foreign Affairs, said that when the war really came the East would be the most dangerous place, specially the South-East. But still James and I stayed on at home and everything was quiet and sunny and we got to thinking the war would never come after all. When every day is just the same you begin to feel that nothing will alter and you can just be peaceable and enjoy it. Thornfield looked very calm and sleepy, so did the Farms, Bell Farm across the lane and Gill Hope up the Hill and Hawksden up beyond the mangold fields that run to the edge of the woods. And the yellow-hammer kept whistling 'A little bit of bread and NO cheese!' to tell you the next day would be fine. Everybody was just the same as ever except that Annie cooked our favourite dinners quite often instead of only sometimes when she was in the Mood and Flora was never cross when we brought mud in on her newly swept carpets. Even Albert, our Gardener, was in a good temper which Father says is always an Ominus sign.

And it was. Because just when we were so sure nothing would happen, the German plane came over. It came over one night at one o'clock in the morning and the sound was quite different from an English plane and we all woke up. You could hear it drumming and drumming like a big bee in a flower, buroom, buroom, buroom, round and round and round in the air above the house and then Father and Mother ran quickly down stairs. Father said 'They're over. It's come at last, Look, the searchlights are after him!' We knew he was peering through the little crack in the blackout we had often used to watch searchlights in the quiet nights.

Then suddenly there were five loud explosions and then six

more and the earth seemed to be running and running under the house and the house trembled and the explosions were thumping in our ears. After that there was a terrible silence and I knew that Father and Mother were looking at each other in the darkness and I felt myself getting small and tight inside. Then Father said quietly 'Meg, they must go!' and Mother said 'Oh, John!' and James and I lay very still and pretended to be asleep when they came up again. We could each feel what the other was thinking but we didn't say anything.

In the morning there was a great enormous Crayter in the middle of Farmer Gadd's cornfield and two of his horses killed, Old Solem and Prince. And Jim Leeves, the Cowman, who was up with Saffron in case she calved, had a splinter of bomb in his leg and had to go to Tunbridge Wells Hospital. We went with William and Walter and Susie Gadd to see the Crayter. The corn was all crushed and fallen round the edge and the hole in the earth was deep enough to put the cow-byre in and there were the horses all bloody and dead and I felt sick. Walter and James went down into the crayter and found some jagged pieces of bomb and kept them for souvenires. And all that day we kept finding things that the bombs had done. There were trees torn up by the roots at the edge of Ratt's Wood and one bomb had fallen right in the river at the bend where the Spindle-Trees grow and one had exploded right on the top of the Bell Farm Oasthouse but luckily there were no hops

6

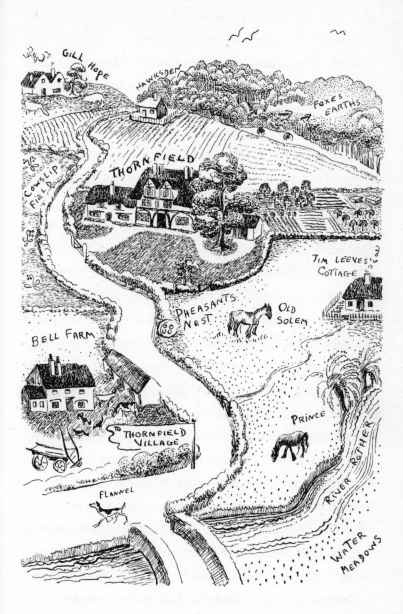

in it. A great many people came out from the Village to see the crayter. And they all said things like,

'I heard un, a gurt long whustlin sound, it were,' and 'It warn't nicely-mannered to drup un on t'crops.' And everybody said it would be bad luck for the German if he came again as we would get him as Sure as Eggs. But Father was very anxious that night and sat up watching. Every time I woke there was a rumble of voices coming from down-stairs and I knew they were planning.

The very next day the cable came from Aunt Harriet in America saying SEND CHILDREN AT ONCE, WOULD BE SO DELIGHTED, SURE IT IS WISEST MUCH LOVE HARRIET and Father and Mother and Miss Minnett went about looking very stiff and straight as though they were thinking private thoughts and did not want them to be known. That was the day Annie let me scrape the pudding-bowl without grumbling though I did not enjoy it as much as usual and Flora gave James her postcard with the Frosted Robin on it and let him help her clean the silver, and Albert actually *asked* us to pick the tomatoes which he never allows generally because he doesn't like children trapezing over his garden. So we knew that we were going and that they were all trying to be kind about it. But what is the good of being kind when you are going to do just what everybody doesn't want?

Father said tonight 'Well, Sabrina, you're old enough now

to take care of yourself and James, too. The proper time to see the world is when you are young.' And he told us how he'd always wanted to be a Cabin Boy and go to sea and see the world. But Mother didn't say anything. Neither did James and I. We do not want to be cabin boys and see the world if there is a war on in England. We want to stay here. But we do not tell them so because their faces will crumple.

... *August*

We are in London tonight staying at Bean's Hotel where Father has always stayed since he was a Boy and his Father before him. The bathroom has a glass screen round the shower and the enamel is not chipped and we have three towels each instead of just one. When you push aside the black curtains you can see nothing but darkness but the cars have tiny shaded lamps and long thin lights like comets stream out in front of them. In Piccadilly Circus they go round and round in the darkness like fish in an Acquarium and as you walk along to the Hotel people flash lamps at you so as not to bump. Once there were old women sitting at the corners selling flowers but now they have turned into men who call out 'Flash, Lady, Flash, Mister, Buy a Flash to show you the way Home.' But Father does not need a flash. He has cat's eyes that can see in the dark perfectly. James says he is Our Father which Art in Heaven because he does everything perfectly. We all held on to him and once he stoped at a Pillar Box and said 'May I help you across the road, Madam?' and pretended to be very hurt when it did not take his arm.

When we got inside the Hotel we could not see for a minute because we were drowned in light. The man at the Counter gave Father two keys, Thirty-Five and Thirty-Four, and asked him how he was after all this time and when he heard about the bombs he just said cheerfully 'Well, there'll be plenty more of those and we can take them all. Yes, SIR.' Then he told Father how Mr Churchill had hit him right in the middle when he said he had nothing to offer but blood and tears and Father said 'Yes, Joe, that's the kind of thing we understand.' But Mother hurried us into the lift after that and would not answer when James asked her why Mr Churchill had to go about hitting people.

James and I like being in a Hotel, specially when we are allowed to work the lift. We would like to live in one with all the family and Annie and Flora and the two ponies and the Mongrel Dog but not Miss Minnett because she is so fussy about manners and her false teeth clap up and down and her stays creak when she breathes. But we can't live here or anywhere in England because we are going away. Whenever I remember that I feel tight and empty as though I were lost.

I have just looked out through a crack and there are

twenty-seven searchlights pointing in the sky and the place where they meet is a little hole of light. You can feel their reflections on your nose when you press it against the window pane. There is an aeroplane high up, circling round and round, but it has a steady quiet sound, not buroom, buroom, so it is one of ours. The door is open between our room and theirs. Mother is sitting on the big bed sewing on Emily's ear. Emily is James' flannel monkey. He does not play with her any more, merely takes her about so that she can See Life. Mother is sewing the ear with great care, bending over it very gently. O I cannot think of her, I cannot think of her.

... *August*

Today has been full of taxis. First we went to the American Consol which is where you write your name on three forms several times and give your age and the address you are going to and that allows you to go to America. On the way we drove over a large hose-pipe in the road and a soldier on guard said it was taking water to a resevoir in the Square so that if a bomb falls on the water-mains there will be planty in the Square. But not to bath with, only for drinking.

A doctor listened to our hearts and looked down our throats and made us say Ninety-Nine and hit our knees with a ruler. When they jerked he said everything was all right.

You cannot get into America unless you can say Ninety-Nine and your knees jerk. Then he asked Mother were we mentally sound and she laughed and said she thought so. But he said it was serious and not a laughing matter and she had better be sure. So she said solemnly she was quite sure but she was giggling when we came out.

Then we had another taxi to the place where you buy tickets. It was full of pictures saying 'Madiera, the Isle of Gold' and 'Come to Cairo for the Winter.' They were all very bright and beautiful. But Father said that they were only baubles and what we needed was the Isles of the Blessed but nobody could get a ticket for those.

He looked over the plan of the ship and bought us the last two berths. The man said they were good ones and above the waterline. We have never been on a large ship before except going to Ireland and I want to be above the water-line. But James wants to be below it and see the ocean rushing past the porthole with perhaps fishes in it or seaweed. But Father said above the water-line was very important and he looked hard at the Cleark behind the counter, who nodded. Their faces are full of Secrets.

After that we had our photographs taken and when they were finished we took them in another taxi to the Passport Office. Here we stood in a cue for two hours because although Father knows an important man in the Passport Office he does not want us to have Special Priviledges.

Special Priviledges are getting in front of everybody else in a cue. 'No Special Priviledges,' he says every time Mother suggests something or somebody, 'They must take their chance with the rest.' And their two faces look like boxes, all shut up, as they always do when they don't agree on anything.

The passports are lovely, pink pages inside and the Royal Standard in gold outside. Mine says Miss Sabrina Lind and James's says Mr James Lind which he has never been called before. They are going to be sewn inside our coats with Aunt Harriet's address and Ten Pounds in notes. James said we could do a lot with Ten Pounds each but Father said not so much as you'd think because that was all we would get till the war was over. You are only allowed to take Ten Pounds out of England and when that is gone you just have to go without. Or save.

After that we had another taxi back to Bean's Hotel and Mother said we could have Anything we Liked to eat no matter how expensive but we were too tired to benefit by it. They want to give us everything they can but we do not want anything, just not to go away.

James fell asleep without undressing and Mother covered him up with the ieder-down and when she had tucked him in she stood there very still looking down at him. And she said My Son. Then she looked over at me and said My Daughter. But I could not say anything only look back at her and feel sick. Then Father came in and said 'Don't, Meg!' and took her out and closed the door.

. . . August

This is our last night at home. It is very difficult to think that we shall not be here any more. It seems as if no place can really exist unless you are in it. But it does because when you go away and come back it is still there living its own life.

Tomorrow we are taking the train for the ship that will take us to America. At any other time that would be an exciting idea. But now I do not like to think about it. Everything is very still. You can hear the horses clumping their hooves in the stables and the snowy owl that nests in the Gadd's barn is hooting on the roof. And away over behind Ratt's Wood there is a high double bark. That is a fox. Or perhaps a vixen. Tonight is like today, very quiet as though it were waiting for something. Everybody has been going about carefully as though they were cups that might spill over.

Father went away this morning. He has been called up into the Air Force but he says we will see him before we go. We went round the stables with him first. Each of the horses has a different smell. You can shut your eyes and tell them by the smell just as you can tell human beings. Miss Minnett smells of rubber and tooth-paste. Mother smells of walnuts and Floris Sweetbriar. Annie has a closed-window smell which is nice out of doors but I do not like going into her room, it is too much. When Father drove away he took Farmer Gadd with him. Farmers are exemptible from war service but since the bombs made a crayter in his field he is angry and wants to volunteer and he has also given the soldiers one of his water-meadows for an Observation Post. There are two big searchlights in the meadow and an air gun with sandbags round it. And today there have been many men down from London in Green Line Coaches to dig out our river. They say if they widen it the tanks will not be able to get across if there is an Invasion. James and I watched them all the morning and twice we tickled trout and caught them. But it was not cheerful because James kept asking me what Mother would do all alone in the house without him or Father if an Invasion came across our river. James is specially worried now about going to America because he has just remembered that in ten years he will be called up and that he ought to be here ready for that. The men who were digging the river said it would not be nearly so long as ten years. Two at the Most they said and they all turned their thumbs up.

In the afternoon we put away all the toys except Wilson, who is a small pig I have really grown out of but of which I am rather fond and, of course, Emily. We tidied the cupboards and Annie and Flora helped and Miss Minnett creaked about telling us about her Sister's operation and trying to be soothing and she let Annie and Flora have tea with us in the Schoolroom. Then we went with Mother to say good-bye to William and Walter and Susie and the Baby. Mrs Gadd looked very anxious when she heard we were going away and I knew she was thinking what about her children too. I wish she could have our tickets and our berths above the water-line for them. Aunt Harriet wouldn't know the difference because she has never seen us and we could help on the farm instead of Walter and William. William gave me his Nightingale's Egg, the only one any of us have ever found. I did not want to take it because it is his Treasure. But he made me.

Now we are sitting still waiting to go to bed. There is nothing to do but wait for tomorrow. It is very quiet and not a bit like a war. We are all very far away from each other, keeping our faces neat and pleasant till we can go to bed. We have both told Mother that we want to go to America, we have told it to everybody. It is easier that way because they can think What Heartless Children and not be sorry for us and we can keep ourselves tight and together. When your face begins to go it just slips and then it goes right off and you cry. James is reading Alice. He has read the same page over and over. I think I will say goodnight to my Dairy now and go to bed.

*

... August

The train is going too quickly for me to write very well. James is holding the exercise book steady on the table while I put my Dairy down in it. Every now and then I look up and when he sees me he looks away quickly to Romulus in his basinette or to Pel writing a letter on the other side of the carriage. But I must begin at the beginning. This morning we left home and we do not know when we will come back but it is no good thinking of that. We drove from Thornfield to London in the car with James sitting on top of the luggage. The hood was down and all the way his hair was flying in the wind and he was holding tightly to the place where his Ten Pounds is sewn inside his coat. Because what if it blew away, where would we be then? We also had our names on linen labels stitched on to our coats. This makes you feel rather public, like a parcel.

There were barriers across the roads all the way, some of them made of barrels filled with cement and some of big concrete pillars like the top of an old castle. Mother had to show her License and Identity Card twice to the soldiers. One of them said 'Coming back?' and she said '*I* am.' 'Not the kids?' said the soldier and she said No that we were going to America and he said 'All aboard for Dixie. Pass!'

It was not quite dark when we came to London and the Barrage Balloons were all up, shining in the sky like silver whales. Everywhere you looked you could see them until we got right into the city and lost them in the darkness. Euston station has great black pillars over the entrance and it is very dark and gloomy. Father says its proper name is Abandon Hope All Ye Who Enter Here even in peace time. It took us ages to get in at the gate because there were cars and taxis coming from every street and trying to squeeze through. Porters were running everywhere being shouted at so anxiously that they could hardly decide who to go to next. James rushed out of our car as soon as it stopped and caught one by the leg shouting 'I've hooked him.' And the Porter was so pleased he'd been hooked that he took every bit of luggage, even Emily and Wilson. Then we walked along by the train looking down the row of windows till we found one that said Sabrina Lind and James Lind on a label. And there suddenly was everybody in the world.

There were Aunt Lucia and Uncle Julian carrying very interesting packages. Uncle Julian is the kind of man who has only got to smile to make you feel better from everything and Aunt Lucia is our favourite aunt because she wears cherries in her hat and is an artist. There were also Great-Aunt Christina and Great-Aunt Betsy fighting as usual except that Aunt Betsy does not really fight but turns the other cheek to Aunt Christina. You feel her neck must be terribly painful bending her cheek from side to side while Aunt Christina is rude to it. Aunt Betsy is very gentle and rather kind but you can't really like her very much. Aunt Christina is much nicer and her bark is worse than her bite. She is deaf and has an ear-trumpet and you have to shout down it. She roared at Mother when she saw us and said 'Late as usual! Hurrump! I think you're a great Fool, Meg, to send them away. Stuff and Nonsense. Perfect Idiocey! How much were their fares, I'll send you a cheque.' Then Aunt Betsy took the Trumpet and shreiked down it 'That will be about Sixty Pounds! How very Kind, Christina dear!' and Aunt Christina glared at her and said 'Shut up, Betsy, and don't Christina me!'

Then came the Cleark who had sold us the tickets above the waterline bringing funny papers for each of us. And after that Pel came, very flurried and laughing and dropping everything as usual, and with her Martin carrying Romulus sound asleep in the Basinette. Pel is our Family Friend. She writes books. After Father and Mother we love her best in the world as we have known her always. And Martin is our Next Best after her. Pel is taking Romulus to America and Keeping an Eye on us too. She makes you laugh and dance inside yourself and at the same time you feel that she is somebody who will always be there and that is a very safe feeling. Father calls her Glorious Pel and Lovely Woman and Angel One but you know that *she* knows he doesn't seriously mean it and that he only thinks she's glorious because she thinks *we* are. He says it with his sweet society face, all turning upwards, but his family face turns downwards and is sadder and nicer and Pel knows he thinks nobody really glorious in the world except Mother and James and me. So she just says 'All right, John, Darling, all right!' very soothingly and then he feels he does not have to make any more efforts. James picked up her bag and Uncle Julian picked up her bunch of carnations and told her she'd be dropping the baby next and she said 'I did. This morning. But he doesn't seem any the worse!' So everybody laughed and the heavy weight in my stomach flew away for a moment. Lots of people came up to say good-bye to Pel and they had loving-cups which are beer in a large mug and James and I had sips from the froth and pretended we liked it.

But all the time I was looking at the clock and thinking Ten More Minutes and then Nine More Minutes and leaning against Mother and not daring to look at her. Then suddenly Aunt Christina roared 'John, John! Here he is! Late as usual!' And there was Father pushing through the crowd and he was wearing a new blue uniform with wings on the sleeves. He looked round and said 'Well, everybody? Aunt Bets, Aunt Christina! Wonderful Lucia, glorious Pell!' But after that was over he took James and me and held us tightly to his sides. I could feel the bones in his leg and the bones in his arm. He looked at us for a long time as though he were remembering every bit of our faces. Then he said – oh, I must remember exactly what he said. He said 'Sabrina and James, there are two things that are more important than any others – Love and Courrage. Will you remember?' He said if we kept that in our minds our going to America would be easy. He said it would be a Weight Off his Mind to have us there while he was fighting. And that he would take care of Mother for us and as soon as the war was over we would all be together again. Then I looked at the clock and there was only one minute more and arms and faces were waving about us but I could only see their two faces for ever and ever.

Then Pel said 'Please Sabrina, please James, carry the basinette into the train for me.' So we left them and carried Romulus very carefully into the carriage. He did not wake up. And then the window was between us and the guard was banging the doors and we leant out and kissed them and the whistle blew. Oh, don't cry, Mother, Don't cry, little one! We will be all right. And Father stood with his face very straight and saluted us and the train moved off and the hands waved out of the window.

We all have a seat each so we can stretch out and sleep. Romulus has not woken up. James is holding the book down hard, his brown fingers are like wet slugs. I pretend not to see how wet they are. Oh, please let us come back soon, please. Goodnight, goodnight, goodnight.

*

Oh dear, what an exciting day. Not the birthday kind of excitement but the sort that makes you feel empty inside and the middle part of you all quivery like a telegraph wire.

When we woke up this morning it was raining and we had a waiter with L.M.S. on his collar and bacon and eggs for breakfast. Romulus was wide awake looking very rosie and we boiled milk for him in Pel's little Tommy Cooker. And then the train stopped. There was no station and we could see nothing but rails and rails running in the rain and beyond them a large shed with two black funnels standing up behind it. Everybody else got out and began tramping across the rails in the rain. We stayed in our seats because Pel said if you waited anywhere long enough somebody was sure to rescue you. And sure enough they did. Two men came and took the luggage and another took Romulus and picked up Pel's carnations. And they weren't porters at all but Rescuers in bowler hats and overcoats. Then we came through the rain to the shed and inside there were people anxiously saying good-bye to each other at the door. There was one man with a long nose who was hugging and kissing a big boy of fourteen. We knew he was fourteen because he had won sixpence from us in the train playing Halma and he told us. It was sad but I would have felt sorrier for the boy whose name is Jacob if he had not insisted on playing for money and won ours.

Well, when all the people who were not going to America had gone, we waited in a long cue because the Evvacuee children had to go on board first, then the Tourists and then us. An Evvaccuee is a child from five to sixteen who is being sent to America or Canada by the Government to save them. They do not have to pay the fare which is very kind of the Government. Well, we waited all the morning and then we had to boil some more milk for Romulus. It is Awful the way babies have to be fed so often. James got very cross at having to wait and when a boy came up and took the toy hen from the basinette James hit him. Then the boy's mother hit James so I pushed her as hard as I could into the wall of the shed. After all, he is only young and childish and she had no right to hit him. Then Pel smoothed it over by lending the boy the hen and she grinned at the mother and said 'What a life!' and they both laughed and it was all right and we began to like the boy.

And then, just as we thought we would have to wait there for ever and never go to America at all, the three men in bowler hats, who turned out to be important Officials in disguise, took us to the front of the cue. They said that Romulus being a baby must not be kept waiting though he had already been waiting for hours. We unsewed the Passports and our Ten Pounds and showed them to the man at the table and he said 'Pass!' Then he asked Pel if she had any diamonds and she said 'Only this and I would rather not part with it.' He looked at her and smiled with two gold teeth and said 'You don't have to. Pass!' And she was so pleased she dropped her carnations again.

Then the Officials led us through the shed and as we came through the big doors we saw the ship. It was waiting there in the water, very still and steady with the gangway leaning against its side. Pel put down her hand and touched the dusty wharf. 'I must feel it once more, just once more.' she said. And we put our hands down too and touched the earth of England for the last time. And so we went up.

When we got to our deck there was a terrible noise of people shouting at each other and running about recognising their luggage and trying to find their cabins. In the middle of the ship was a blackboard saying 'All Passengers are Required to Carry Life Belts all the Time.' And just beside it at a long counter called the Purser's Office people were waiting in a cue to complain that they had been put in the wrong place. But we did not have to complain because we were in the right place in a cabin above the waterline with the porthole covered with boards. Outside there is a black arrow and a sign saying 'Follow the Arrow for Lifeboat Station D. Six Blasts or Over Indicates a Lifeboat Warning and Thereafter All Passengers are Immediately Required on Deck.' Pel's cabin is just opposite ours and when we went into it we found a very old lady sitting on one of the beds. So we came out very quickly and Pel said

'Never mind. After one night with Romulus she will very likely move and then we will have it to ourselves.'

So we went on deck and watched the luggage coming up in fishing nets and a sailor rescued James from being beheaded by a cabin trunk that fell out of the net by mistake. At last when all the luggage had been put in the right cabins and we had had lunch, there was a long blast on the ship's funnel just like the roar of a bull and the gangway was drawn up and we began to move. You could look down and see the little thin line of water grow wider and wider as the ship went gently out into the water. Jacob came and stood beside us because we were his Only Friends. And he cried. But we stood close to Pel watching the shore slipping away and the soft green hills behind it. Pel said that we would keep that line of green in our hearts till we came back to it.

And just then there were Six Short Blasts on the funnel so we ran to our cabins and tied on our lifebelts and Pel tucked Romulus inside hers as he is too small for one of his own. Then we followed the Arrow and it led us to the top deck. Everybody else was there fumbling and tying and asking if it was a Torpedo and in the middle of the noise Pel dropped her purse and a steward trod on it and she shrieked 'My Mirror! Seven Years Bad Luck!' But it wasn't broken after all. So then we stood in rows waiting and the ship moved on into the still water and James suddenly said 'I can swim. I can swim half a mile. I can dive off the top mast. I can do the

Crawl.' And by that you knew he was frightened because he always begins to boast when he is frightened. But a steward told him there was no need for that today because this was just Drill and we could now take off the belts. So James felt relieved and we all went down to supper. On the way we heard the Old Lady complaining to the Purser about having Romulus in her cabin. And another not quite so old but wearing gloves and a hat was saying 'This is a horrible ship. My cabin is a Disgrace. I want to get off and go home. I never wanted to come, anyway, but my Daughter insisted. Could you ask the Pilot to take me off in his boat?' But the Purser said No, he was very sorry but he couldn't because once you were on a ship you were on for good. And the lady went away with weeping and nashing of teeth.

After supper we came to bed. James has the top berth. Emily and Wilson are in it with him. He is having both tonight because he feels rather small. Before we came in from the deck we wished on the first star.

Star light
Star bright,
First star I've seen tonight,
Wish I may
Wish I might
That the wish may come true
That I wish tonight.

I cannot tell the wish, even in a Dairy because it is unlucky but it is about the war and Thornfield. I told James I had invented an idea tonight and it was the idea of choosing a star every night and saying goodnight to Them on it. And he said 'Well, it is funny, I have invented that very same thing. So I will do it too.'

The ship is making a very enginey noise and it has begun to shake a little. So now I will go to sleep. I hope I shall not always feel as empty as this.

... *August*

It is a funny feeling to be going to America on a ship that is not going to America. All day we have been standing quite still in the water and you can see the green shore looking as smooth as though a hand had stroked it and in the distance there is more land, dim and shimmery and lavender-coloured. Even if we knew the name of it I could not put it in the Dairy because Pel says it would be censorible. The green shore and the sunlight and the blue water remind me of Ireland where we go in the summer to stay with Grandfather. There are shrimps under the rocks and curraghs to sail in and when the clouds are down on a particular mountain it will rain and when they are not it will be fine.

Ever since we got up we have been watching the land and the aeroplanes marked with English markings that come swooping over the ship and then up into the sky again. Behind us there are seven other ships waiting to sail and near them are three destroyers and a battleship. This is a Convoy. Our steward, whose name is Appleton but James calls him Appletart, told us that an Armed Merchantman is also coming with us. This sounds more protective, somehow, than the others but Appleton says it is not.

Also we have met two new friends called Thomas and Susan Mercury who are lucky because they are travelling with their Mother who is an artist. This means painting and drawing and sculping but not writing. The way we met them was that Thomas dropped his knife over the rails and it fell into a Lifeboat and James climbed over into the Lifeboat and rescued it. And now everybody is talking about it. There are a lot of old ladies sprinkled about the boat and they all keep saying to each other 'Did you hear about the little boy who got into the Lifeboat? It's Propesterous. The Captain should be told. All these children are really running wild. It is shocking.' They are also saying that they will complain at being held up all this time and the one who wanted to go off with the Pilot and whose name is Mrs Birdie keeps on standing by the Purser's Office even when it is closed saying 'Monstrous, monstrous. I insist on being put Ashore.' But Appletart says there is no hope for her unless she jumps over and swims.

All the people on this ship are women and children

except a few foreign men with large noses and very short legs who do not speak very good English and always sit on the soft chairs in the lounge so that everybody else has the hard ones. There are three hundred Evvaccuee children who climb all over the ship and make a terrific noise and have a lovely time and keep the babies awake. James and I have made friends with several of them. We keep our autograph books in our pockets in case we should meet somebody important. We have only got one name so far, Mrs Patience, who is the oldest person we have ever seen and therefore important for an autograph. She is the one who does not want Romulus in the cabin because she says she can't sleep. But Pel said she snored steadily for seven hours last night and that should be enough for anybody. Mrs Patience shows us her picture postcards and the photographs of her Great-grand-Children and says the Stewards and Stewardesses are a Disgrace and that she has never known such a dirty ship. But Pel says they are not really. It is only because there are so few of them and all the rest are needed in England and we are very lucky to have any. Then Mrs Patience sniffs and says that Pel can be a Martyr if she likes but she has paid Cabin Fare and therefore expects Cabin Amenities. (These are comforts.) She wears a white woolen Tam-o-shanta and about seven coats because when you are old you feel colder. And over them all she wears a tartan rug.

The short-legged foreign men have taken all the deck-chairs though they are only Tourists so we lie on the deck on rugs with our Lifebelts for pillows because we must never leave them behind for a minute. Nor babies either. A very cross man with gold ribbon on his cap came roaring down the corridor this morning and said 'Who belongs to that child in the pink coat and black perambulator on the lower deck?' And Pel said 'If it's the one with the absurd nose I do.' And he said 'Woman, what will you do if we are torpedoed? Hadn't thought of that, I suppose? You must not lose sight of him for *one second*.' So Pel said meekly that she wouldn't and he said Hump and went away.

That is why we have to have Romulus down to meals though he always puts his foot in the spinach. We take it in turns to hold him so the others can eat and sometimes a very pretty lady who sits at the next table with Mrs Birdie takes him and gives us a rest. So does the doctor who sits at our table and is telling Pel the story of his Life. It is not very interesting because he did not begin as a Cabin Boy but only as an ordinary doctor and he took a long time to pass his exams because, he says, he is stupider than he looks. The story is also about the wife he has just got and is therefore rather fond of and he will only be able to spend three hours with her when the ship docks as he has to come back with the Convoy. When he told her that part Pel said that the worst thing about war was not the hardship and the labour but the separations of people who love each other. And I looked at James and knew that we were both thinking of Thornfield. Oh, what are they all doing now? Mother will be quite alone tonight. She will be sitting in the big white chair in the study with Mouse (who is a cat not a mouse) on her knee and she will have her folded away brooding look that makes her seem so small and loveable. She will be thinking of us out on the sea. And here we are not even moving. There is no way of telling her not to think of us on the sea and be anxious. We cannot get to her anywhere. O dear darrling! I have told James we will have hot baths tonight. When you have a hot bath everything changes and is smoothed out and perhaps tonight we won't remember so much when we go to bed.

. . . August

The ship is moving. It is rocking sideways and up and down and the waves are hurling themselves against it. We cannot see anything because the porthole is boarded up. I have been sick three times and James has been sick five times. Pel cannot afford to be sick because she has to look after Romulus and bath and feed him and wash the napkins because there are so few stewardesses. But still she is sick all the same. An Apple is supposed to be good but it doesn't really help. Neither does Celery or dry toast. I cannot sit up to write in my dairy tonight because when I do there is a weight running round and round in my head. Besides there is really nothing to say about sea-sickness, you can only feel it. The ship is going up and down very giddily. James has just been sick again.

... *August*

Today is sunny and calm and the ship is lolling about in the water and we are lying on deck being careful to move as little as possible. Thomas and Susan have been sick, too, but not so often as James which makes him very proud. Pel brings us Oranges and Apples and then lies down again quickly. She says that tomorrow we will all have our Sea Legs but James thinks as he has been the illest he may not get his till the day after.

On board ship you are always being told great secrets and then you discover that everybody else knows about it too. Today we heard that the reason we were held up so long before setting out was that there were U.Boats (German) outside in the Ocean and we had to be screened by a fishing fleet as well as our Convoy. Everybody got very excited about this and sat a little closer to their Lifebelts. And whenever we feel able to sit up we keep an eye open for U.Boats which can be recognised by their Periscopes. But there is never anything but ocean and no land anywhere though aeroplanes keep coming out and swooping over us as though they were keeping watch. Behind us the other ships follow in a semi-circle and the destroyers move backwards and forwards among them. But the Battleship goes along beside us because we are the first ship of the line. It is long and thin and lies very deep in the water and its silver shape cuts the sea in two. We can see sailors standing by the guns and every few minutes a different set of flags runs up the mast and lights flash signals all day long.

Whenever James looks for U.Boats he begins shouting 'I can row, I can row with one oar. I can work an oxiliary motor and I like hard tack and bully beef.' And by that you know he is a little frightened that something may be going to happen. Pel knows too. So she began to tell us a story about a Desert Island where a group of people were wrecked, quite nicely wrecked in a calm sea and more because they wanted the adventure than because of U.Boats and Torpedoes.

She tucked James into the rug on one side of her and Romulus on the other and went on and on in the drowsy voice she uses when she is really enjoying a story. And suddenly it seemed to be quite true and as though it were really happening. There we all were on a wooden raft, using Thomas' shirt for a sail and Susan making soup from bully beef on the Tommy Cooker. James was trailing a mackerel line which he had been thoughtful enough to bring with him and I was opening a tin of Hard Tack with the knife Father gave me last birthday. Romulus was there, too, but travelling in a more romantic manner as his prambulator was being drawn over the water by a sea-horse who every now and then threw up his head and neighed with Pleasure. Presently James shouted 'Heave ho, my Hearties, land ahead!' and we saw the outlines of a Coral Island shining in the sunlight and smelt the aromatic scent of tropical vegetation and Thanked Heaven for our delivery. It was no time, Pel said, before we had skimmed over the intervening waters and passed the breakers and were sailing safely in a calm Lagoon at the edge of which was a golden strand strewn with Cocoanuts and festooned with a great variety of natural Flora, particularly Palm-trees. We had just got to the part where Thomas leaped overboard and courageously pulled the raft to shore and James was asking if *he* hadn't jumped overboard, too, just as courageously, when the gong sounded and we had to go carefully down to tea.

It was then that we heard on the Wireless that bombs were falling over England and James was sick at the table in case some might have fallen on the South East and Pel was very white. But she said sternly that none of us should think that way and that we had to remember what Father had said about Love and Courrage and that we would not listen to the wireless any more.

Then she put James to bed and gave him some tablets and

soon he stopped thinking and dropped off to sleep. When she said 'Do you want some of the sleepy medicine too, Sabrina?' I said No. Then she gave me a long look, the kind that goes right inside you and knows what you are thinking. She said 'Women, Sabrina, have to watch and pray.' Then she went into her cabin and brought back Romulus all curled-up and sleeping. 'Take him into your berth for tonight.' she said and kissed us both and went away. So he is here beside me now very warm and cuddly and I am writing carefully so as not to waken him. He has a sweet milky smell. I will sing to him very softly the song Mother used to sing to us.

> Matthew, Mark, Luke and John,
> Bless the bed that I lie on.
> Before I lay me down to sleep
> I give my soul to Christ to keep.
> Four corners to my bed,
> Four angels round me spread,
> Two to foot and two to head
> And four to carry me when I'm dead.
> I go by sea, I go by land,
> The Lord made me with His right hand.
> If any danger come to me,
> Sweet Jesus Christ deliver me.
> He is the branch and I am the flower,

Pray God send me a happy hour,
And if I die before I wake
I pray that Christ my soul will take.

This is a good song for very young children and rather comforting.

. . . August

Today has been a lovely day, all wild and blowing and full of gayety. In the morning Pel came in and took Romulus and said 'Get up get up, Mystery is afoot. I do believe, Children, that old Mrs Patience has jumped overboard. Her bed has not been slept in!'

So we dressed quickly and Pel said that directly after breakfast we must search the ship. Then we ran downstairs because we now have our sea-legs and told the Doctor about Mrs Patience. 'What!' he said. 'Overboard in that white Tam-o-Shanta and the seven overcoats? Impossible.' But he thought we were wise to search the ship and asked us to let him know the result because if it was true he would probably have to do something about it.

After that we looked into the state-rooms along our corridor and she wasn't there. And gradually we were able to get into all the lavatories and she wasn't there. James said she might have changed from First to Second Sitting so we went back to the dining-room but we could not see her. Then we looked round the decks, just in case, though she never goes on deck because of the cold. And all the time we were getting more excited because there wasn't a sign of her. When we had looked in the Bar, which she never goes into, and the Smoking-Room and the Writing-Room, Pel said we'd better give it up as the poor old lady must have gone over the rails. Pel said she felt particularly sad because Romulus must have been the Direct Cause. But we did not feel at all sad because, after all, Mrs Patience had had a pretty long life and left lots of Great-grand-Children to keep her memory green. James and I decided we had better go and tell the Purser and he could put the news on the Notice Board the way they do when they want you to leave your Gas Masks or put your Clocks back. James thought it would be best to say 'MRS PATIENCE GONE OVER-BOARD MUCH REGRETTED' but I thought 'IN LOVEING MEMORY OF MRS PATIENCE ASLEEP IN THE DEEP' would be better.

And then, when we got to the Purser's Office, what do you think? There was Mrs Patience sitting behind the counter looking older than ever and playing Solitaire. James said 'O!' in a disappointed voice. 'So you're not dead!' And Mrs Patience looked up and said 'Certainly not.' 'Then where did you sleep last night?' said James. 'We've been looking for you everywhere because we thought you'd gone

38

overboard.' 'In the Lounge.' said Mrs Patience. 'On a sofa. I couldn't stand that child gurgling and cooing and growling every morning from six o'clock onwards. People should have their sleep, it's Disgraceful!' That made James angry and he said Yes, it was disgraceful because Pel stayed awake nearly all night on purpose to stop Romulus gurgling and growling and waking up Mrs Patience. 'Well,' she said, 'she needn't any more because I am staying with the Purser for the Time Being and later on he is going to find me another cabin. Would you like to see the photographs of my Great-grand-Children?'

But we had seen them all so often and they are all ugly so we said No Thank You and went away very disappointed in Mrs Patience. But it is a lucky thing she has gone all the same because now Pel and Romulus can have the stateroom to themselves and we can go in and out whenever we like without Mrs Patience asking us to wait while she dresses. Dressing with Mrs Patience only means putting on another coat. Pel says all this has Cleared the Air and it must be true because I often see her having whiskie and soda with Mrs Patience before dinner and they both enjoy each other very much.

After that we went on deck and watched the destroyers leaving us. They only come out for a few days to see the ships safe on their way and then go home to escort others. They turned away in a very ceremonius manner and the rest of the Convoy steamed up closer to us, moving slowly and carefully as though it were a dance. The lifeboats hanging from their rails made curving black shadows on their sides and the long shadows of the ships stretched out over the ocean and green water trailed out behind them.

I was leaning over the side watching the ships suddenly I heard Mrs Birdie give a little scream and said 'Who is that Boy in the rigging? Look, look! My Goodness he'll be down the funnell in one second.' And I thought – James! And it was. He was being brought down by a sailor from the funnell where the air comes through and when they both got to the bottom he shouted 'It's lovely up there, Sabrina, you can see everything, down or up!' Mrs Birdy said 'Outrageous. That Boy should be horsewhipped.' And the Sailor said in a grim voice that James would probably see a good deal more than he liked in the Captain's cabin. He took him hard by the arm and hustled him along the deck. I followed them because if James was going to get into trouble I would have to be there. But Thomas and Susan were coming up the ladder just then and when I had got past them James and the Sailor had disappeared. I looked and looked for them and at last I went up the ladder that says NO ADMITTANCE CAPTAIN'S QUARTERS. And there was James in a little room on the Bridge all glassed in like a conservatory. He was working an enormous wheel. 'I'm steering the Ship, Sabrina!' he shrieked. 'This man is

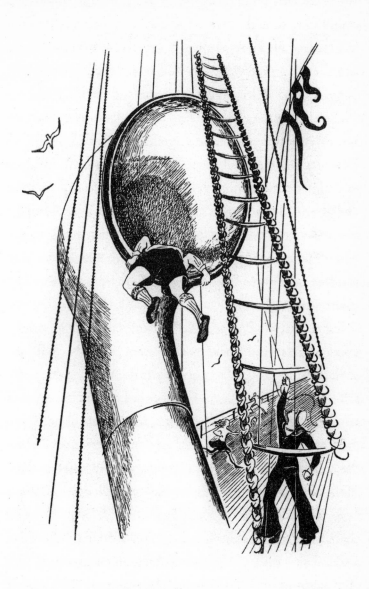

the First Officer and I have promised not to go in the rigging again and I'm steering the ship!'

Then the First Officer, who is a tall man with blue eyes and a face thrust forward as if he were looking for something special, let me stand behind the wheel and take the spokes in my hands. And when I steered the ship quivered in the wheel and I could feel the trembling of the ocean run into my hands and on to the top of my head and under my tongue. The First Officer said 'Where would you like to steer to, Sabrina?' So I said 'Home.' And he said 'Well, that's where we're all making for though we have to go a long way round. This route is as good as any.' And his face went forward and far away again watching.

After that Pel came up the No Admittance ladder because she says those are the two words that are absolutely certain to attract everybody. And the First Officer and also the Second Officer (who has a thin brown outside face with no secrets) fell in love with Romulus and they stood him on his little naked feet and made him steer the ship, too. Pel said 'Be careful, or he'll steer us into Eternity.' But the First Officer said that didn't matter as we were all making for that anyway. Then the two Officers signed their names in our autograph books and the First pointed to a man in a blue jersey on the lower deck and said 'See that fellow down there? Go and get his.' I asked if he was important and the Officer said 'Certainly. He's an Able Boddied Seaman.'

So I took James' book and mine and went to the little forward deck where the paravenes are kept and the Able Boddied Seaman turned out to be very nice and wrote his name twice. 'But don't tell any of the others,' he said 'or I won't be able-boddied any longer.' Then he let me help him splice a rope and asked me my name and if I was like my Ma. And I said 'Well, she has a small deer's face and she looks shy and young and enquiring and as if she didn't want to be hurt.' 'Then you are like your Ma,' he said 'and what are you going to do when you grow up?' All old people ask that but I didn't mind the Able Boddied Seaman. So I said I might be a First Officer or perhaps a Clown in the circus because I like both but perhaps I would rather have some children. About six boys with one or two girls sprinkled in. Girls wriggle their bottoms and always stop the game just when they are going to be He. Then the Able Boddied Seaman gave me a nice piece of tarred rope which I shall always keep in memory of him and he says if we are wrecked he will send Mother a consoling message in a Bottle.

When I got back James was with Thomas and Susan. They were making drawings of ships and lifeboats and people which they do very well because their Mother is an artist and James was writing one of his poems on the ship's writing paper. It goes—

The Unicorn
At early Dawn
He blows a blast
Upon his horn.
Oh, children, hear him
All forlorn
Blowing his horn
The Unicorn.

I think it is a nice poem and he does, too, and he is going to send it to Mother for her birthday.

After that we went down and had a very large tea to make up for all the meals we had missed. Pel persuaded the Steward to give us ices though they weren't on the menu because with Mrs Patience found and the Steering of the Ship and James' poem it was a day for a Treat. Then we went with the Evvaccuees to see a Donald Duck picture and felt full and happy. I have wished on the first star. Goodnight.

. . . August

Today has been a dull day. The sea makes you feel sleepy and there are large patches when you do nothing and feel cross. Then you have a meal and do nothing again. And feel crosser. The only people who never stop doing anything are the Evvaccuees. They wake Romulus up and then we have to leave what we were doing and push the pram.

Still, today had one good thing in it and that was Finding a New Friend. This morning we were walking down a corridor with Pel and we looked into a cabin and there was a girl sitting on a bunk crying. Not sobbing, just big tears running slowly down her face on to her hands. And she was not attempting to blow her nose either. So Pel, who cant bear to see anybody cry, went in and asked her what was the matter and the girl said she didn't know. 'As Bad as That?' said Pel and the girl nodded. Pel gave her a handkerchief and James and I sat on the other berth and watched her blow her nose. The sobs came right up out of her stomach for a little while, then she said in a teary voice 'I think I must be Omesick.'

'Oh, dear' said Pel, 'that's how we all are!'

So we all cried a little which was better than only one and Pel took us back to her cabin and we had Eau de Colougne behind our ears and sniffs of smelling salts which made us sneeze. Pel said, 'Well, it can't be helped. Let's forget all that and have a pillow fight.' So we did that and the electric light was broken and we felt releived.

The little girl said 'Coo, I dont Arf feel better, do you?' She has black hair and a very rosie face and never says H if she can help it but why should you bother with Hs anyway? Pel sat down panting and asked her what her name was and she said 'Ripe. Gwendoline Mary-Ann Ripe.' And Pel laughed and looked at her rosie cheeks and said 'Are you sure it's not Cherry? I shall call you Cherry Ripe, anyway.' And the girl grinned and said she didn't mind if Pel did. Then she told us all about herself.

It seems that though she is only aged eleven she is the eldest of a large family that lives at Stratford-Attey-Bow, London. Her father was an Engine Driver which made James envious but when he heard the father had been killed in a train accident he was sorry. Her mother gets a pension, which is a little money that stops when you are dead, and she makes some more by Scrubbing and Washing. After Cherry come Bill, nine, Alfie, seven, Lou short for Louise, Lilly with a cast in her eye and the Baby, Bertie. When the war began to be bad their mother's cousin wrote to her from America saying he could take one child. He is called Uncle Ernie and keeps a shop and has reumatism something terrible.

'So', Cherry said, 'We talked it over, Mum and me, and it seemed like we ought to send one of the boys. But Mum said they'd be no good travelling by theirselves and anyway the Government would probably evvaccuate them to the country so we thought it ud better be me. But I don't Arf like it all the same. She's never ad to get on wivvout me and Ow she'll do it now I simply don't know. That's a fact.'

And her rosie face began to crease up so Pel said hurriedly we would all go on deck and find Thomas and Susan.

They were there wheeling Romulus up and down and Cherry was so happy to have a baby again that she was not a bit shy.

Pel said to me 'We'll adopt her for the voyage so she wont be lonely and we'll find a place for her on the Raft and eventually on the Desert Island.'

That is just like Pel. She does everything her own way without asking anybody else if they would like it. And now she thinks she can just adopt whoever she likes and put them on our Raft and everybody else is expected to say 'How lovely!' I told her that her face looked just like the face of a little girl who has done something wrong. Surprised and hurt.

She said 'But, Sabrina, how would *you* like to be so lonely?' But I told her I did not think I would be with a cousin called Uncle Ernie who keeps a shop. Specially if it were groceries and I could weigh the sugar. And anyway, what would she *do* on the Desert Island? There are quite enough girls as it is. 'O,' said Pell, 'we'll find use for her. And she needn't worry you at all. She can stay beside me and be my Devoted Christian Slave.' Then I said I would rather it was me being the Devoted Christian Slave because that was a very nice thing. And Pel said 'So you shall. We shall all be each other's Devoted Christian Slaves because that is how things work.'

After that I felt better and not so cross and I began to like

Cherry very much. So do the others. She wears very brightly coloured dresses and she enjoys herself so much that *you* enjoy her, too. Besides, she helps look after Romulus because, having brought up so many babies, she knows a lot about them. And that is a great consideration.

Mrs Mercury is making a picture of Cherry but she insists that Cherry does not talk while she does it. She gets tired of so many voices and faces everywhere and says 'If only One could be by Oneself for half an hour!' But that is impossible because wherever you go there are voices and faces. She and Thomas and Susan have another old lady in their cabin so she is never alone. I like Mrs Mercury. She has a gentle quiet voice as though it were coming from under water and when she is not laughing she has a watchful look that seems to be trying to find out about the inside of things. She said 'I know. I shall go and do some ironing and be alone in the pantry.'

Then James and Cherry and Thomas and Susan went off to get autographs. But I am rather tired of autographs so I sat on the rug all the afternoon rocking Romulus and watching Pel sleeping. I am frightened when I see grown-ups asleep. They look as though they had forgotten everybody and gone right away into themselves. I feel that perhaps they will never wake up again and we shall be left quite alone and I kept going close to Pel to make sure she was still breathing. She has a very small breath just like Mother's. No sound at all and hardly a movement. Mother makes me very anxious. Sometimes when she is asleep I am afraid she is dead and I think of it in the night. Once, when I woke up, I thought of that and went into her room. It was dark and very still and I was afraid to go near the bed. Then I saw James in his pyjamas standing close to her and he said in a whisper 'It's all right. She's breathing.' And I knew then that he had the same thoughts as I did and we went away quietly and held on to each other very tightly and did not say anything.

While I was remembering that, Pel woke up and smiled her curly smile and said 'Well, have you been watching me and discovering all my secrets?' And I was so pleased to see her wake that I flung myself down and hugged her. 'Oh, Pel, Pel, I'm so glad you're alive. I do love you.' Then she sat up and looked at me for a long time without speaking and her face was sad as it always is when she is not smiling. Then she said 'You have a full cup, Sabrina, and the thing to do is to learn to carry it without spilling over. Nobody can help you, you have to do it by yourself. And it takes time, I am only learning it now.'

I could not understand what she said. Or rather, not with my head but I seemed to understand it in my stomach. She put her arm round me and we sat looking at the sea going up and down beside the railing of the ship and it was very peaceful. Presently Thomas came and said 'I've seen a Dolphin!' And James said 'I've seen two Dolphins!' And

Cherry and Susan had seen seven. So we all went to look for dolphins and there they were leaping in and out of the water like black shooting stars. And after that we went down for supper and to find Appletart to get his autograph. There he was sitting in the steaming pantry with his coat off. Pel asked him why he didn't sit somewhere cooler and he said that everybody liked their own bit of a place and she said that was true. So he signed his name and made a sweaty mark and then he blew the hair out of his eyes and began to sing and the more he sang the more he steamed and sweated. He sang a song called *The Wretched Mrs Dyer*, all about an old lady who was unkind to many babies and another called the *Ten Thirty Train*. And then we sang *Shenandoah* with him and *Way Down Rio* and soon everybody in the corridor was singing, the Doctor and the Bath Steward and Jacob and even Mrs Patience. It was lovely. When you sing you feel all the things you don't want inside you coming out and all the things you do want staying in. But just as we were finishing *The Daring Young Man* Mrs Birdie rushed out of her state-room looking very violent and crying 'Have you no mercy? Silence. I beg you. This ship is nothing but a Menagery.'

So Pel hurried us away and the Doctor said 'All lions and tigers into their cages at once!' and he chased us down the corridor hissing at us to be quiet.

So now we are in bed and my crossness has all gone. The

light must go out now so I cannot write any more. Only this. Goodnight. We never forget you.

... *August*

Today the wind has been blowing very hard. From the Pole, the First Officer said, and you could imagine it sweeping over Greenland's Icy Mountains and ruffling the fur of Polar Bears before it got to our part of the ocean and knocked us over every time we stood up.

So we spread the rugs and life-belts in a sheltered place and Pel said it was no good trying to do anything and that we had better all lie flat and go to the Desert Island.

In one minute we were back at the place where Thomas and James were beaching the Raft and when it was secure we all sprang ashore. The strand was warm under our bare feet and a gentle breeze rustled the palm trees and knocked down ripe cocoanuts. Thomas and James immediately set to work to make a fire and as Cherry had been thoughtful enough to bring a box of matches in a rubber sponge bag we were all happy to be able to benefit from the Amenities of Civilisation.

At that moment the wind blew Mrs Mercury down the deck and she collapsed on to the rug and asked what we were doing. When we told her she wanted to know if *she* couldn't somehow get to the Island, too, because there she might have a chance of being alone. 'You'd better hurry, then,' said Pel, 'because the ship is sinking rapidly.' But Mrs Mercury said that was of no consequence as she was a good swimmer so she immediately dived off the side and presently arrived on the strand very wet but not even breathless. She was hardly dry before the First and Second Officers were blown along, and when they heard where we all were they said couldn't they come, too.

'Can you swim?' said Pel and they said of course not because they were Sailors. Then she told them there was a small collapsable rubber boat hidden under the Companion Way. So they got it out and blew it up and presently they were skimming over the ocean with the British Flag streaming out behind. 'I spy land!' said the First Officer, looking through his telescope. 'Thank God, we're saved!' said the Second. Then they manouvered the boat into the lagoon, sprang ashore lightly and, having planted the Flag, sang both verses of God Save the King. We all ran to welcome them and offered them slices of roast sucking-pig and some delicious ale made by boiling dates, yams and pig's trotters together.

'But we haven't had time to get all that food yet!' began James. 'Shut up, James! Do you want us to die of starvation?' said the Second Officer. Then Pel put it right by saying that Mrs Mercury had stuck the pig with my penknife and Susan had roasted it to a Turn and she herself

had climbed the trees and got the fruit for the ale. 'You two boys,' she said to James and Thomas, 'had naturally to be on the look out and keep an eye on the Officers in case they turned out to be Pirates.' So James was molly-fied and we all rushed around cutting down trees for a log cabin. Luckily Mrs Mercury had brought an axe and a saw in a sailcloth bag on her back when she swam from the Wreck. In no time we had made a beautiful log-cabin with palisades round it against native murauders and a few comfortable chairs made by the Second Officer who was very good with his hands. By that time it was night and we had supper of pig and yam soup out of oyster-shells, gourds full of cocoanut milk, and fried fish that James had caught on his mackerel line. In all Pel's stories there is plenty of food and very good food. Because she says that a person who doesn't enjoy food has something seriously wrong with their other senses. And after that we all retired to bed weary but rejoicing in the knowledge that the day had been usefully spent and confident that the Morrow would bring forth further opportunities of proving ourselves worthy of our Fortunate Lot.

Then it was lunch time but nobody wanted to break the spell. The wind howled round the funnells but we were warm and safe on our Island. So Pel had sandwiches and soup brought up by the Steward who was bowled along the deck to us as though he were a ball. And when Mrs Birdie came up to take a little air her hat with the feathers was blown off but not away as it was fixed to her head with elastic. Cherry said 'Coo-er!' and that made us laugh but we did it quietly and Mrs Birdie did not hear. She just looked furiously at the wind and went down again hurriedly.

'Now, let's get back to the Island.' we all said. And the First Officer said 'Yes, we must get back. To the Island. Back to the centre. Oh, hidden beneath the palm tree, under the running water, under the Turtle's wing, at the still point of the turning world, oh, hidden!' And Pel smiled at him with a recognising look and said 'T. S. Eliot.' The First Officer nodded and seemed more anxious than ever to get to the Island so he could talk about T. S. Eliot who, it seems, is a Poet. Then Mrs Mercury took out a pencil and began to draw and when we asked her what it was she said 'The Still Centre' but when we said 'The centre of what?' she only laughed and shook her head and would not say.

Then Pel began the story again and we were back inside the log-cabin. Suddenly the quiet was broken by shouting and singing and sounds of Frightful Glee and round the bend of the Island came a hoarde of Natives armed with spears, their bodies painted with fearful and mysterious signs, their heads crowned with helmets of rabbit-skin and their waists incircled by belts of Venemous Snakes. As they drew nearer they danced and waved their spears and from the noises they made we gathered that they wanted a white child for supper, particularly a milk-fed child, fat and very tasty. All eyes turned to Romulus, peacefully sleeping in the prambulator while beside him the faithful sea-horse munched dried sea-weed from a little manger Thomas had made him. It was an Awkward Moment.

Then Pel said somebody would have to take their courage in their hands and hold parley with the natives and who would volunteer? James said 'I will. I can Hold Parley. And when I have parleyed with them they will slink off and never come near us again. Pel, they aren't *very* fierce, are they?' James is the kind of boy who *sees* everything you tell him. He sees it in pictures inside his head and sometimes he is frightened. So Pel said that James really must wait for her to finish what she was saying and that what she had been going to remark was that there should always be *two* people holding parley. And that if he really wanted to do it the Second Officer must go with him. They were to open the door just a crack and talk ferociously through it.

So they did that and suddenly everything came right because it turned out that the natives did not want to eat Romulus, after all. They had outgrown cannibalism through the Benevolent Ministrations of a Missionary who had once stayed six months on the Island. This kindly man had also taught them to speak excellent English and they told James and the Second officer that their sole object in visiting us was to give us a Rousing Welcome. So, much relieved, we flung open the cabin door and hurried out and the natives shook hands all round. The transports of delight that followed Pel said were too splendid to relate in ordinary words and must be left to the imagination. Then we gave the natives some date ale and they gave us a large Water-Melon each. After that they insisted upon offering us the Freedom of the Island and carried us off on shields to their Settlement in the heart of the jungle. There we were greeted as Gods and Heroes by multitudes of happy self-effacing children of nature. They slew a wild ox in our honour and having roasted it before our eyes cut off the best steaks for the Great White Family. After that we sat around the camp fire till nightfull listening to the Head Man's stories and eating figs, Alligator pears, mangoes and bananas with unflagging appetite.

But with darkness a change came over the natives. They broke into a series of war-cries and seized their spears and shields and began to dance, stamping their naked feet on the sand and uttering wild and improbable cries. 'What kind of cries?' said James, 'Fierce and Brutal?' No, said Pel they were of a cheerful, and complimentary character. At last the natives cried themselves hoarse and fell in an exhausted heap at the side of the fire so as a Reciprocal Courtesy the two officers very kindly agreed to perform a Sailor's horn-pipe which they danced with great elasticity and abandon to the delight and edification of All Concerned. By this time the night was well advanced and it was time to go home so the natives loaded us with gifts, nuggets of gold wrapped up in Banana leaves, spears and daggers of the most delicate flint, necklaces of ivory, shark's teeth and pearl, and we returned triumphantly to our simple shelter. Thereafter we decided to pitch our cabin beside the mud huts of the natives and there we dwelt with them in the pleasantest conjunction, marrying and intermarrying, eating and drinking and laughing and singing. And the stars stood up in the sky and the sea lay still at our feet and Heaven rained gifts upon us and the earth brought forth fruit and we all lived Happily Ever After.

When supper time came the wind swept down from the Pole and the deck rose up so that it seemed like climbing a mountain. But the cold did not freeze us because we were still warm from the Desert Island. All the evening we could feel it, even when Jacob won another sixpence from us through insisting on playing Rummy for money.

We went to bed after that and when he was in his berth James said 'I wish we really could, don't you, Sabrina?' I said 'What?' And he said 'Live Happy ever after. You know, sometimes just for a minute I feel all by myself. Even when I was at home I felt it. And I feel a bit frightened.'

So I told him to come down into my berth and then he would not be alone. And he did that. And presently he began to make up a poem and forgot about feeling frightened. James can forget very quickly. He is still so young.

... August

This morning at breakfast Pel said to the Doctor 'Have you ever noticed that every journey seems to be divided into two halves? Up till today we have been coming from England but this morning the change has come and from now on we will be going to America.'

It seems a funny thing to say but in a way I feel it, too. All this time I have been thinking at the back of my mind that something lucky might happen and we could go back. But today I know it won't. We cannot go home now.

The wind is not coming from the Pole any more and there is no Desert Island. This is one of the days when grown-ups shut themselves up in their own world and keep you out. They are just the same outside and they laugh and talk and do things with you but inside you know they have forgotten you. I think there must have been bad news on the Wireless last night because Pel and Mrs Mercury and the two Officers stop talking and look hard at each other whenever we come near. 'Go and find something to do!' they said and when we told them there was nothing they said Nonsense that there was always something to do on a ship, why not get a ball or hunt autographs or play shuffle-board.

Once I heard Pel say burstingly 'Oh, it's awfull to be away and not taking it with the rest. We're missing our rightful experience and losing our lives by saving them. I am afraid they will speak another language when we go back.' And the Second Officer said 'But what about the children?' And she said 'There are children left behind. I must think of them too. And anyway, it's always the children from generation to generation. We are always cashing cheques on the future, never living in our Now.' 'Well, even so,' said the First Officer in his quiet voice, 'if you've chosen to do it you might as well do it calmly.' And when he said that the fierce self-look went out of her face and it was gentle. She said 'Yes, you are right.' And she smiled at me when I sat down near her and I knew she had come back for a moment. But all four of them went on sitting on the rugs with closed faraway faces as though they were asleep with their eyes open. Pel said, 'It's the earth I shall miss, quite apart from human relationships. It is necessary to me. I feel that my body is made of the woods and rivers.' And I knew she was talking about England and sat very still for fear they would notice me and send me away.

The Second Officer was not listening to anybody. He said 'We must smash Berlin, give them some of their own back. That'll learn them!' And the First Officer said 'Reciprocal brutality? That won't give us a new world.' 'No, indeed,' said Mrs Mercury 'but a new world we must have. The old one will not do.'

I wondered what the new world would be like and if it would look the same as the old, with the hills in their own places and the same people going about and Thornfield standing where it has stood for nine hundred years. How can anybody make a new world who is not God?

Then the First Officer said 'We'll have to be remade ourselves before we can remake the world. It is we who must be renewed.' And he went on talking quietly with his face pushed forward and searching and they all sat very still and listened to him. He said 'It's not only Germany. Germany's a symptom. The war, as I see it, rises from a sickness in the very heart of humanity. We're all tainted with it and we must cure ourselves before we can hope for peace.' They all nodded and the Second Officer made a shooting movement with his arm and said 'Smash Berlin. Have at them, all the same!'

But the First Officer didn't notice him. He just went on talking and saying that England would have to stand and take it and stand until everything was worn away except pure spirit. He said 'Damn it, it's our chance of life and our opportunity as a nation. It's what we've been waiting for and unconsciously longing for, this purifying fire. Of course, I'm only a sailor and no good at saying things. But I bet the poets and artists would agree with me.' Mrs Mercury gave a twisty smile at that and said 'If there's anything left alive in them vital enough to agree.

It's the hardest thing in the world to say Yes.' 'But the only word for an artist.' said the First Officer and Pel nodded.

'Of course you're right,' she said. 'That's why I want to be there and the worse it gets the more I shall want it. It is like being wounded in one's own body.' When she said that I knew that there really had been bad news last night. And I was even more certain when the First Officer said 'Make no mistake, it will be worse than this. This is only the beginning. There is much more to come. But we can take it.' And when he said that a proud unbreakable look came on all their faces.

Then suddenly the Second Officer jumped up and said 'Good God, look at that boy!' And there was James leaning backwards over the railing of the ship so that his feet were hardly even touching the deck. The Second Officer and I ran down the deck and caught hold of him and he said 'Oh, Sabrina, look at the kites!' He leant back again and I saw that there were great white box kites swinging from the mast that has the crowsnest on it. And presently other kites climbed up to other masts and danced in the air, waving and flapping. 'Are the sailors having a day off for kite-practice, do you think?' said James. But the Second Officer told us that the kites were like the barrage balloons over London, put there to catch enemy aeroplanes. And when we looked over the sea we saw that every ship in the

Convoy had kites riding from it on invisible wires, even the battleship. That made us all very excited because there is something about a kite flying in the air that gives you a happy dancing feeling inside you, as though you were part of the kite. Cherry said 'Coo, you should of seen my Dad fly a Kite. Old the string on the end of Is finger, E would, and orf it would go like a Sparrer. No, a Neagle. E was a champeen kite-flyer. Once E got a medal for it on Ampstid Eath.'

After that we all got paper from Appletart and made kites for ourselves and flew them from the deck till it was time to go down. It was because of the kites that I forgot everything the grown-ups had said till I came to bed tonight. But now I am thinking of it again.

I do not want a new world. I want the old world with everything in its own place and no changes. Oh, why can't they be peaceful and leave things as they are? Well, if they can't, perhaps they will overlook Thornfield, a little place like that might easily not be noticed. We will go back again and find it the same as ever with the pear-tree that the lightening struck and the white stone over the well and the crooked doorway and the old sagging stairs. And the same faces will be waiting for us, quiet and happy, Oh, do not change anything. Do not alter it or make a new world. Let everything be always the same for ever.

*

I woke up very early this morning because James was talking to himself. Then he shouted down to me 'Sabrina, wake up! I've got another poem. Listen.' And he said

> 'If I had a star
> Out of the sky
> I'd light a fire with it
> To make toast by.
>
> If I had a moon
> I'd hang it on a tree
> And cover it with leaves
> So it couldnt see me.
>
> If I had an angel
> With a blue wing
> I'd sit him on the mantelpiece
> And make him sing.'

And Just as he had finished Pel came softly in in her dressing-gown all curly with sleep and said that writing a poem was the loveliest way to begin a day and that we must celebrate it by going on deck to see the sunrise. So we all went upstairs in our dressing-gowns, tip-toeing so as not to wake Mrs Birdie. There was nobody else up there and the floors of the deck were wet with spray and in the grey light the black funnells of our ship were beautiful and ghostly. The other ships of the Convoy were dark shapes on the water and behind them was a little crack of light at the edge of the sea, like a mouth opening. We leaned over the rail and watched and soon the crack grew wider and a rosie light began to shine round the edge of the clouds. I could hear James holding his breath because he had never seen the sun rising before and when I looked at Pel she seemed to be looking further away even than the sunrise.

Presently Mrs Mercury and Thomas and Susan came up the ladder and leaned over the railing beside us and after them Cherry in a chrimson dressing-gown with a yellow collar. Nobody said anything and the light rose and rose behind the clouds as though nothing could ever stop it. The glow of the sun came across the water like a long road of light and touched the side of the last ship in the Convoy and then the next and then the next till at last it climbed over the side of our ship and shone in our faces. Pel nodded at the sunrise and said 'England's over there. She is now the place where the sun rises.' And I thought of the green shore and the sun coming up behind it. 'Look!' said Pel and there suddenly was the sun itself standing quite clear of the sea and turning the grey water to gold. 'We ought to be celebrating.' said Mrs Mercury. 'We should be drinking wine or eating great bunches of grapes.' 'Wait!' said Pel and flew away down the deck with her dressing-gown streaming out behind her. In a little while she was back saying 'I couldn't get grapes but the Second Steward gave me Peaches. They're almost as good.' So we leaned over the rail and ate the peaches and spat the stones plop into the sea and the sun came up and up. Then it was bath time and we had to go but all day it seemed as though a very special sun was shining because we had watched it rising.

After breakfast there was a cloud on the other part of the horizon that turned out to be land. 'Look!' said James and when he pointed we saw the Paravanes swinging out from each side of our ship. Paravanes are for catching mines and preventing them from blowing up ships. We were not afraid. Nothing terrible can happen in the sunlight. But soon all the ships of the Convoy came up slowly behind us in the form of a horshoe with the ends opening to the land. And when that was done the Battleship moved a little way ahead of us. Pel watched it for a long time and said how faithfully it had protected us and brought us safely over the ocean.

'It has been a wonderful voyage,' she said. 'I expect the Pilgrim Fathers said that as they were coming in to harbour.' And she told us that we were modern Pilgrim Fathers sailing to an unknown country and not knowing when we would see England again. It was then that James burst into one of his rages and said he did not want to go

to an unknown country and that the only kind of Pilgrim Father he wanted to be was the kind that goes back home. He said he would know hardly anybody in America and that the faces would be different and the boys would wear different clothes and there would be no place to sit still in and be himself. By that Pel and I knew that he was frightened but Pel would not pet him. She was quite stern and said that if America took him in and cherished him he must take in America, too. She said you couldn't refuse any experience or say No to life and that anyway he was lucky to be going to America at all. She said that it was a very friendly and peaceful country and the fact that it was different from England made it more exciting. She told about the Mississippi River which is so wide you have to cross it in a ship and a place called Charleston where the black-green cypresses stand up in the black-green water as mysterious as the Arabian Nights and New York where the buildings are like great tongues of flame turned to stone. James stared at her and said 'Go on!' and she told him that the American air makes you feel alive and lively and how there are squirrels and chipmunks and woodchucks in the woods and in the forests mountain lions and bears. And about the great mountains and deserts and the Indians with their ancient secrets. And that it wasn't Christopher Columbus who first discovered America but a man called Leaf Erickson who landed there and ate wild grapes in the sunlight. 'Go on!' said James but Pel said No, that that was enough for the present. So he said 'I will take America, Pel. I will take it right in.' and she called him her Golden One and dropped her purse.

All day we were moving gently towards the land, which is Canada. The ships went very carefully through the water because of mines and everybody was quiet. Except Mrs Birdie who was very snappy when she heard that Pel and Romulus and James and I were going by aeroplane to New York. She said in a loud voice to a lot of other people 'Don't ask me to believe they can do *that* on £10 each. They must have brought more, probably a whole hoard. It is against the law and somebody ought to Tell the Government.' James said 'But—' and was just going to tell her that our flying tickets had been bought in London before we left when Pel stopped him. 'Don't tell her,' she whispered, 'she will enjoy reporting us so much.'

Tonight the ship is hardly moving at all, just a gentle swish down by the water-line and no sound of engines. You can smell the fir trees. Tomorrow we will be landing. In a way I do not want to leave the ship. I have got used to it. But we cannot stay long anywhere now. And perhaps when I am on land I shall feel closer to Thornfield. The sea is very sep-arating. Goodnight.

*

. . . August

We have arrived on land. This morning when I took my hairbrush to Pel she said 'We've tied up!' We did not know that because our porthole is still boarded. So she brushed me and said,

> 'The loose train of thy amber-dropping hair,
>> Sabrina fair'

which she always does when she brushes me and it is by a poet called Milton. Sabrina means the Severn River, Sweetest of Waters.

Then we went on deck and sure enough we were tied up along side a wharf with a large building on it. And there was the land of Canada all covered with dark green trees and smelling like Pine Tar Shampoo. I was disappointed to find it so small. I thought Canada was covered with Rocky Mountains. But it must be a nice place because Dan, our Milkman, went there once to Seek his Fortune.

The morning was very exciting because everybody on the ship was packing and the stewards were taking away the trunks one of which nearly fell on James when he darted under it to rescue a Ludo Counter. Appleton said 'If that boy gets to his destination alive, it'll be a marvel.'

Pel packed for us and we began helping her but after a while she said that if we helped any more she'd go Stark,

Staring Mad and probably put Romulus in a trunk by mistake. So we collected Cherry and went upstairs to find the lobby full of trunks and suitcases and people sitting on every stair wearing hats and gloves and suitable land clothes. A Steward told us we should be off the ship before lunch and that we'd better cue up. Then Pel came up carrying Romulus and dropping the Passports and after her Thomas and Susan with Mrs Mercury who gave one look at all the people and said 'Good God.' and turned back. But Pel assured her nobody could get out of it. So we all stood and the cue grew thicker and thicker and hotter and hotter and nobody knew why they were there. At last by shuffling along we got to the Children's Nursery where we saw three very stern men without coats sitting at a table among the rocking-horses and play-pens. At last it was our turn and we sat down in front of the sternest man and he asked us why we had come. Pel told him because there was a war on and he said 'Hum.' quite fiercely. Then he asked us our names and ages and where we lived and where we were going and put it all down on three large sheets of paper. James said 'They asked us all that at the American Consul and the Ticket Place and the Passport Office and at the wharf when we left and again on the Boat. Wouldn't you think they'd know it all by now?' 'Oh, dear, no!' said Pel. 'It takes longer than that to grasp it. These are Officials.'

Then we signed our names and when Pel signed hers

71

Romulus kicked the pen out of her hand and suddenly the stern man laughed and took Romulus himself and said in a very kind voice 'Welcome all, to America!' though we were not even in Canada yet. You never can tell with a stern face. They often turn out to be the nicest.

We spent all the afternoon in the cue. At six o'clock Pel said Romulus must have something to eat but the Steward told her the dining-room was closed and there was no more food. Then Cherry said 'Arf a Mo. I got an idea.' and pushed back through the cue and we thought she was lost. But presently she was back with a packet of Biscuits for Romulus and sticks of Chocolate for everybody. She had been to the shop in the Tourists and bought the last. That is just like Cherry, always giving somebody something. Pel said 'Oh, Cherry, your *dear* money!' but Cherry looked away shyly and said 'Wot's it for but to spend? You can't let Bibies starve.'

Then suddenly the cue began to move and we shuffled down the gangway at the foot of Which was a tall soldier with blue eyes who offered to carry our things. So we gave him the most precious which were Romulus and Mrs Mercury's wood-block and James exorcise book of poems and suitcases of Thomas and Susan and Cherry and he carried them to the next cue which was rather a nice one because it gave us Biscuits and Tea out of a large jug.

There were soldiers everywhere, sitting on bunks

whistling and winding their puttees. They said 'Just wait till *we* get there!' and they were so strong and handsome that we thought England would be all right once they arrived. Then the cue moved on and we told the story of our names and ages again and then we ran down through tunnels till we came to the platform. A train was waiting there and a black man in a white coat took our hats and put them in large paper bags. But Cherry said 'Not mine, Us Government children's going by another train.' Her face creased up as if it was going to cry and she said 'I don't arf want to leave you, seems like me own family, honest!' I simply could not bear the thought of losing Cherry because she belonged to us now. So I hugged her and we promised to write and James gave her one of his half-crowns and she kissed us all hurriedly and darted away. But Pel said 'Wait for me, Cherry!' and the two of them walked down the platform together talking and presently Cherry lifted her head and smiled and flung her arms round Pel for a long minute. Then she went into the tunnel and we did not see her any more.

Thomas and Susan and James and I got into the train and looked after Romulus while Pel and Mrs Mercury collected the luggage. They came back after a while with the First and Second Officer and we had a sending off party with a delicious drink called Coco-cola for us and whiskie-and-soda for them. We were all excited and gay but I do not like to think we will not see the Officers again, particularly the First. Then they both got out and the train went off quite suddenly, not with a great bustle like an English train but just a bear-like growl and away.

Now we have had our first meal in Canada and are very tired. When we came back to our carriage we found all the seats had changed into beds with curtains. You sit on your bed and undress as well as you can and put your clothes in a little hammock by the window. They are called Pullmans and there is ice-water in the taps. James is on top and he keeps calling down and saying 'Sabrina, we're in Canada, our first foregn country.' As if I didn't know. It *is* rather exciting but Canada is a long way from England and it is raining and no stars to wish on.

. . . August

All day we have been travelling through Canada in the train. We are very tired and none of us like each other very much and the noise is even worse than the ship. We sat in the Observation Carriage watching Canada rushing past. There were lakes with water lilies and farms with simply acres of corn on the cob which made our mouths water because it is so hard to grow in England. And after that there were trees and hills and rivers going on and on and we just looked at them and felt cross with each other and very hot. Then Susan suggested that we should all draw pictures of the least pleasant person we knew. So we drew Mrs Birdie Through the Ages and hating her made us like each other again specially when James drew the first picture, which was God Creating Mrs Birdie and she looked just like a catter-pillar.

After a long time the train stopped at a little station and we got out to stretch our legs. On the platform which was made of grass instead of stone there were rows and rows of children, some kneeling and all holding up their hands, with a large Policeman standing by. Pel asked him what all the children were there for and he said in a very respectful voice 'Why, Mam, to do honour to all of you.' Pel said 'Good gracious!' and dropped her handkerchief which the Policeman picked up. He told her then that he had suggested the idea himself so that the children here could greet the children from England. And Pel said he couldn't have thought of anything better and he seemed pleased until he noticed one of the boys secretly putting out his tongue at James. James put out his tongue too so after that we felt better and less important.

All the afternoon the train rushed through Canada as though it were eating it up and the forests ran along side us echoing to the train whistles. They make a deep sweet roaring sound that goes on and on till you think the woods must be full of hundreds of musical bears.

And now we are in our Pullman beds. I can look out and see the moon. As there is only one moon in the world it must be shining over Thornfield too and Mother will be looking at it and thinking of us. Because today we sent her a cable from a railway station saying 'Arrived safely, Love, Love, love.' The man who took it said that if we only put one Love it would be cheaper. But we said No. Pel sent one to Martin but she only put Arrived because she said that said everything. It is funny how cables make you feel very close to the people you send them to. Goodnight.

... August

Now we are in Montreal, where all the streets seem to tip up a little. Pel says they don't really, it is only because we have not got our land legs. We arrived before breakfast and saw the houses standing up among the trees and that gave me the feeling that now we would be able to stay still for a bit. There were several black men dressed up as Porters and they took the luggage and Romulus and called him Rommy. Then suddenly Mrs Mercury and Thomas and Susan left us because there was somebody to meet them and James and I wished we had somebody to meet us if it was only Miss Minnett. But at that moment a large number of people dressed in blue with scarlet coats swooped down the platform and said they were the Red Cross. One of them came up to us and smiled and said 'For goodness sake, what a beautiful baby!' and she took Romulus from the Porter and asked Pel if there was anything she could do for her. Pel said 'Well, I haven't any Canadian money and I wonder what I do about Porters.' So the Red Cross Lady gave Pel a Canadian dollar which was worth four shillings before the war but goodness knows what now and Pel gave it to the Porter. The rest of the Red Crosses met the Evvaccuees and gave them drinks of tea and asked everybody their names and ages. We told them ours, too, and all we could think of about England because Canada belongs to England and they naturally want to know all about it. Then just as we were looking for a Taxi our own special Red Cross said Nonsense, that she would drive us to the Hotel herself because she couldn't bear to part with Romulus. So we all went in her big grey car, swooping and hooting round the corners. It was very nice to see buses and trams again and people walking about as though nothing terrible were happening in the world.

When we got to the Hotel, which is just like a Cathedral inside, Pel signed her name for all of us and the Red Cross looked at it and said 'My goodness, you must be – well – are you really – Goodness, how lovely! You must come home to lunch with me and bring all the children and meet mine and call me Letty and never, never return that dollar! What luck!' Which was all very exciting because now we had a Freind, too.

77

Then a man with brass buttons brought us up to an enormous room with three beds and a cot in it and a bathroom that was all mirrors so you could see yourself wherever you looked and Letty said she would send somebody to amuse Romulus while Pel rested. But when a Red Cross did come it was Pel who was amused because the Red Cross had to tell her all the latest news that we couldn't get on the ship and Pel had to tell her what had happened before we left. And by then it was time to go to lunch so we got into a taxi and drove up a steep hill lined with trees and grey houses. Pel had got some Canadian money for her English pounds but when he heard we were English the Taxi-Man would not let her give him a tip. By the end of the conversation he did not even want to take the fare but we made him because of his living.

Letty's four children are boys and this was a great relief after so many girls. One is very tall and one very small and a fat and a thin one come inbetween. They said O.K. and Gee and Scram and chewed gum just like the people we have seen on the films. We chewed gum, too, until it began to taste of rubber when we spat it out. We stayed there all the afternoon playing till Letty's husband who is a famous doctor called Kent came in and said 'Hello there, Kids! Up England!' He has the kind of face that makes you want to keep on looking at him. Very kind and twinkly and it seems to say to you 'There now. Everything is all right. Don't worry.' He gave us all cocktails of lemonade and coco-cola and took us for a ride in his car to show us the river spreading out like a fan at the foot of the hill. At the end of the drive Pel asked him to stop at the Cathedral because she wanted to burn candles. So she and James and I went in and there was water in two enormous sea-shells, very beautiful and fluted. We are not Catholics but Pel said there were so many people burning candles for us in every sense in England that it would be nice to burn some for them and for our safe arrival. So James and I bought one each and burnt them for Mother and Father and Pel bought two but she did not say who they were for. It is very hard to think up a prayer while you are in church though they often jump into your mind at other times. When we came out James said 'Did you pray, Sabrina?' and I said No, because I couldn't think of one. But he said he could and that he had been very preempertory with God because he was taking such a long time getting this war over.

Then Kent and Letty brought us back to the Hotel and we had baths and went to bed. Romulus is asleep and Pel and James and I are sitting up in bed eating bowls of bread-and-milk which a waiter wheeled in on a table large enough for a banquet. He stood fiddling with the silver and napkins until Pel gave him twenty-five cents to go away. Foreign waiters, she says, are like all the Murderers in Shakespeare, they burst in on you at any unexpected moment and have to be bribed before they will leave.

I wonder if our candles are still burning, all alone there in that big empty church, protecting people. They are such very small lights. I suppose they *can* do it.

... *August*

This has been one of the most special days in our carreers. Because now we are in America and between here and Canada we have had an Extraordinary Adventure.

In the morning Letty came with presents for us and a gardenia for Pel and then we took a taxi to the Airport with Mrs Mercury and Thomas and Susan. On the way we discovered that the taxi-man's name was Jim Donovan, and what do you think, he comes from Dunfanaghy in Ireland which we know so well. And he wouldn't take a tip, either. At the airport we told our names and addresses and ages again and felt very tight with excitement because we had never been in the air before. James said 'I shall like it. I am a very good Flyer. I shall not be airsick.' And you knew by that that he thought he might be. Then suddenly there was a roaring sound that grew louder and louder and there rumbling across the field towards us was a silver plane. A voice that came from nowhere said very loudly 'Take Your Seats, Please. Montreal to La Guardia Airport, New York. Take

Your Seats, Please.' So then we had to say goodbye to Thomas and Susan which was difficult because we may not see them again for a long time and a lady who looked like a Cinema Attendant in a little cap and blue coat hurried us up the gangway and showed us our seats. The aeroplane seemed very small inside. Pel made Romulus wave his hand to the Mercurys and then the door shut and the engine rumbled and a little light in front of us said 'NO SMOKING FASTEN SEAT BELTS'. Then with a terrible roar the plane ran across the field and when I looked out of the window I saw that the earth was falling away beneath us. 'We're up!' said Pel. We looked down and saw Mrs Mercury and Thomas and Susan waving and then we turned and flew higher and saw them no more.

Presently Pel unbuckled the belts but I was afraid to move in case I over-balanced the machine. The earth seemed to be growing larger because it was spread out so flat, with the rivers and lakes and trees and hills lying very still upon it. Then the Cinema Attendant brought us milk and biscuits and by the time we had eaten them we had gone so high that there was no more earth only thick white wool everywhere like the back of a lamb and the sun was shining on it. What do you think, it was clouds! They looked just like the snow last winter when the pipes burst.

Presently one of the pilots came through the little front door to talk to the Attendant and he stopped beside us to ask us our names and ages and where we had come from. He said we were flying very high to get out of some bad weather. When he had gone James decided he would be a Pilot when he grew up and I almost gave up the idea of being a Mother. It was then that the man sitting next to Pel asked if he could take photographs of us all. So he did that and afterwards he held Romulus and had a very peculiar argument with Pel all about Gold. He said that America had all the gold in the world which does not seem quite fair. But Pel said it didn't matter as the gold was all locked up in a hole in Kentucky and it wouldn't do America any good anyway. He said Yes it would, a Hell of a lot of good because after the war she would lend it to all the other countries to buy American goods with. Pel said 'Not England. We're not going to borrow it. We're going to have a new Economick.' 'Lady,' said the man, 'there is no such thing. You'll have to borrow. You won't be able to help it.' I could see Pel hadn't the proper answer because she looked so furious. And the man just laughed the way they do when they think women are rather silly and tactfully said that Romulus was the handsomest baby he'd ever met.

'It's getting dark,' said James. 'That's because we're coming down.' the man told him. And presently rain began beating against the windows and our ears were singing. Everybody peered through the mist trying to see where we were going. Then suddenly the plane turned and made a loud drumming noise and we found ourselves in the sunlight again with the white clouds rolling beside us.

'Must be a low ceiling,' said the man. 'He can't find an opening in the clouds.' And he kept pulling out his watch and putting it back again. And all the time we kept darting down into the rain and up into the sunlight again with a lurch. 'We're hours late already,' the man said and James said 'I think I shall be sick soon.' But Pel hurriedly asked for some more biscuits to keep him from thinking about it.

And still the plane did not come down and everybody was getting very furious with the Cinema Attendant. At first she said she could not tell them anything but later when the pilot had been through again she said that there was no ceiling at La Guardia and we were going to land at a place called Floyd Bennett. Soon after that we came down into the rain again swinging from side to side very frighteningly. Then suddenly I felt as though I were in a lift that was falling too fast and James shrieked 'I see some land' and the earth seemed to come sloping up quite close to us. There was a terrific bump and our ears sparkled and there we were running along the field, safe and sound. The man beside Pel said 'Well, that's a relief. I was just planning how I could possibly throw myself in front of all four of you when the crash came.' 'Was it really serious?' said Pel and he said 'Lady, it was the most serious moment of my life. And I've seen some moments.'

Then he lifted us all out of the plane and took us to the Restaurant. This time Pel hadn't any American money so he bought us coco-colas and Romulus some milk and Whiskie-and-soda for Pel and himself. He also gave her an American dollar in Case of Need and said not to return it because we had all been such an experience for him and anyway, it was part of the first Gold Instalment. We sat drinking under some palm-trees and trying to make out what America looked like but it was too dark. Then suddenly there were lots of voices calling 'Here they are! Pel! Pel!' And Pel gave a little cry and said 'Oh, *darlings!*'

Everybody was talking at once saying Welcome and how lucky it was that we were down safely and one of them was a lady in a tweed coat and crinkles in the corners of her eyes and Pel brought her over to us and said 'Here they are!' and it was Aunt Harriet. It is very difficult to meet an Aunt for the first time but we did not need to talk much because Aunt Harriet did it all. She said I was like Mother and that James was like Nobody she could think of and how much luggage did we have and if we were ready we would put it in the car and be off.

And suddenly I felt tight and lonely and I did not want to be off and leave Pel. I could not say so but Pel understood. She gave me a long look and left the others and came with us all to the car. Aunt Harriet talked all the time saying how were Mother and Father and that she hadn't seen Thornfield since she was a girl and she hoped it hadn't changed because it was so lovely. And suddenly I got the idea that she was talking so much because she guessed what we were feeling about Pel and wanted to make it easy for us. And I knew we were going to like Aunt Harriet very much. 'I'll take good care of them, my dear!' she said to Pel and got into the car and Pel put her arms tightly round us and whispered 'My golden ones, Love and Courrage. I'll see you very soon.' And she stood waving to us in the darkness till somebody came out and took her inside again.

Then the car started and there was dark country rushing past us and Aunt Harriet telling us all the things there were to do in America and after a long time we turned in at a gate and drove up to a large white house gleaming with lights.

James jumped out wildly and said 'Quick, quick, draw the curtains! You've forgotten the blackout.' But Aunt Harriet caught hold of him and tucked her arm through his and said 'Why, James, boy, we don't have the blackout here. This is a safe place. This is America.' Then a man's voice called out 'Hiya, kids! Welcome!' and it was our Uncle George Seaton. There were also Georgina and Washington, who are sort of cousins and faces floating round us asking how we had left England.

'Now, now, tomorrow will do. They are worn out.' said Aunt Harriet. 'They must go straight to bed and have supper there.' Which was very understanding of her. She brought us up to two bedrooms with a bathroom in between and there are zebras painted on the walls and woven into the towels and the Bath Mat.

Now we have had supper and Aunt Harriet has tucked us in and told us how glad she is to have us safely here. We like her very much. And now we are really in America at last. O Goodnight, Mother. Do not be anxious. We are quite safe and happy. Quite. *O Goodnight.*

PART II

'I GO BY LAND'

... *September*

I have not had time to write in my Diary lately because there has been so much to do. Aunt Harriet said we must just settle down and relax after our adventures. But even the days she thinks are quite dull are as exciting for us as special days in England. Each one is different and it seems to be over almost as soon as it is begun. This is because Time goes so much faster in America. I suppose it has to do that to keep up with England which is five hours ahead. Sometimes it goes so quickly that I hardly know where I am. I get lost in it and have to say my name over and over to myself 'Sabrina, Sabrina, Sabrina' which always brings me together again.

When we first came the woods round Uncle George's house were yellow but now they are slowly turning red as though each tree was catching fire from another. There are fields beyond the woods and a little river that runs over a waterfall into a large lake. When we have time we are going to explore them all.

Today Aunt Harriet bought me an American hat and a new dress in the Village. In Miss Pigeon's store at Thornfield you can only buy prickly woolen underwear and men's overalls and pink things for Babies. But my new dress is as beautiful as if it were bought in a city. It is blue embroideryed in yellow and the little hat is scarlet and turns up all round. Also it is covered with very small elephants and rabbits and ships and horseshoes and birds and there is a little bell on the top that jingles when you run. I wish Mother could see it. It is just the sort of little hat she would love. It is like a fairy story and I will tell myself one about it when I have time. But it is hard to invent stories when you are living right inside one. You know how you feel when you turn the pages of a very exciting book? Well, America is just like that.

. . . September

Today an awful thing happened. We became destituted.

Uncle George asked us did we want any money but we said No because we still have a good bit of our Ten Pounds. He looked very serious at that and told us that our Pounds are no good any more because the British Government won't let us spend them except in England. 'Never mind.' he said. 'While you are here I will lend you some dollars and after the war we will all come and stay with you and you can lend us some pounds to balance things up.' Which was very kind considering how precious dollars are. That is because they will buy so much more. If you spent a whole dollar on

Candy (which is chocolate and caramels and chewing-gum) you would get enough for a month. But, of course, that would be a Wartime Extravagance.

Uncle George has a very solemn face when he is not laughing. When he laughs it breaks up into creases and he shakes all over and goes 'Uh, uh, uh!' But when he is not amused it is rather a sad face that has never got what it wants. You never have the feeling he is at home but just somebody sitting in a very clean room waiting to go somewhere else. To his Office, I suppose, which is Oil. Not Olive or Castor but Petrol. He is always tidy and never wears a dirty old coat. Father has many dirty old coats and he always turns back the right sleeve from his wrist very eligantly. James does it, too, so I suppose he is his Father's Son.

Aunt Harriet is quite different. She is at home everywhere. Uncle George is outside but she is right inside and quite settled. She is a very Affectionate Nature. She likes people so much that she cannot stop doing things for them. Early in the morning she makes plans and she is still making them late at night. In this way nobody else has to decide anything for themselves. James and I are always so interested in the plans that quite often we don't get them done in time and then she has to make others. You have to keep on running to keep up with Aunt Harriet. She is like the Red Queen but much prettier and her face is all crinkled with smiling, like a fern. She uses Eau de Cologne behind her ears and has lots of tweed coats with the right hats and gloves to match.

Georgina is called after Uncle George because Aunt Harriet is so fond of him. She is thirteen and getting breasts. She tosses her head proudly like a horse and her hair is curly with a permanent wave. She thinks we are rather young but James tells her we cannot really be young because we come from the Old World. 'Pooh,' she says, 'New Worlds are much better!' She laughs at him and tweaks his hair but he likes her very much and carries things for her.

I wish I could get some breasts.

Washington is her brother aged seventeen. He is called after his father, too, who was called after George Washington, the great old American Statesman who would not tell a lie about his hatchet. Usually he is just called Wash or Washy unless people are proud or cross with him. He is very tall and vigourous and his face creases up like Uncle George's. I like men very much. Much better than boys. Washington is almost a man. He laughs at the way we talk and calls it Pidgeon English and he says we are Cute Kids but not Vital. But that is only because we have not got used to being vital yet or perhaps we are vital in another way. He is very envious of us because we have seen bombs and when he is grown up he is going to be a pilot in the Air Force.

Nelly, the Housemaid, wears black dresses and has trouble with her teeth and Kate, the Cook, wears white with a red cheerful face. Micky, the Chauffeur comes from the County Clare in Ireland and his son Patrick is one of our best friends already because he has three ferrets and we are going ratting with him. He is also a Champion Spitter and is teaching us the Long Spit, the Drop Spit and the Over-the-Shoulder.

Being with Uncle George and Aunt Harriet is like having a whole new family all at once. It is a very useful idea and prevents you from feeling so lonely. I expect Mrs Dionne felt like that about getting Quintuplets.

. . . September

One of the best things about America is the way you do not ever have to wait for anything. For instance, if you want ice you have only to go and get it from the Referigitator. We have never had a Referigitator at home, only blocks of ice that Mr Tanner, the United Dairies, brings out every second day, except Sundays when he hands round the Plate in Church. Here we can have ice cream several times a week instead of waiting for a Birthday or Easter.

Also you can have a room hot or cold in a minute. Today Aunt Harriet said to Nelly 'Please send some heat up to Sabrina's room.' I ran upstairs at once just to see and there was the room quite warm, like a bird's wing. Sending the heat about like this is almost as good as being God. It is as if God said 'Let there be heat.' And there was heat.

We went shopping in the Village today with Aunt Harriet. It is not a bit like Thornfield where it takes the whole morning to go to the Baker's and the Grocer's and the Chemist's and the Post Office. In Aunt Harriet's village you do everything at one shop or at the most two. You buy meat and vegetables and fish and sugar and cigarettes all in the same place. And next door there is a Drug Store which isn't really so much for medicines as for Ice-cream-sodas or, betta still, Coco-cola. Coco-cola is the best food in America unless you count corn-on-the-cob. Aunt Harriet says if you drink too much it Goes to Your Head but we have never had too much yet. Unfortunately.

Everybody in the shops talked to us and asked us about England and how many bombs we had seen and if our house was all right and whether we were frightened. And we told them all we could. And when we were in the Drug Store having just one more Coke (American for Coco-cola) a lady with a long thin face under a very smart hat came in and said 'Well, Harriet, how are you and these are your little Refugees, when did you arrive children and what was the trip like, it must be terrible in England everything in flames, how old are you both and where do you live, they must come up to dinner on Sunday, Harriet and tell me all about it, I can't wait now, were there any bombs dropped on you and did you have a proper shelter, poor little things, I hear the shelters are frightful, they seem quite well-fed, Harriet, dear, dear, it is all so terrible, how much are the tooth-brushes?'

She went on and on talking and James and I went on and on looking at her, saying nothing but thinking that we did not like being called Refugees and Poor Little Things. After all, we have Thornfield in England and Uncle George and Aunt Harriet in America and what more could you want? I knew Aunt Harriet knew what we were thinking because her smile crinkled hard at us and when the Voice had to stop to drink an Ice-cream-soda she said in a polite bitter voice 'Thank you, dearest Molly, it is *so* kind but Aunt Porter is coming on Sunday. And Sabrina and James are *not* refugees, dear. Try and remember. They are the children of my Girlhood Friend, Margaret Lind, and they have come to America to be our Guests for the Duration. So Goodbye, dear, Lovely to see you.'

Then she pushed us out of the Drug Store very quickly, and when we were in the car James said 'We couldn't be Refugees, anyway. Refugees are people from Poland and Belgium who wear shawls and have soup in sheds and no home anywhere.' Aunt Harriet said 'Of course!' And he was so pleased with her he wanted to give her something special, his cowboy suit if she liked.

But she thought it might be a little on the small side, as of course it would.

But that wasn't the whole day. This afternoon a boy came to tea and in the middle of a piece of cake he asked us if we had seen any bombs. We told him we had and all about the crayter. Then he said 'Well, you don't have to worry because England will get on all right once America is ready. We'll win the war for you.'

Of course, I knew he was only saying that because he was mad we had seen the bombs and he hadn't. But James got very red and then very white as he always does when he is angry so I gave him a Warning Kick under the table. Then on top of that what must Burton (the boy) do but ask James his favourite game and when James said 'Cricket' he said Cricket was a sissy game and that no American would be seen playing it. It was then that James stopped eating and asked Burton to come outside.

When they got back Burton was crying and he had a big blue bruise near his right eye. Aunt Harriet gave a peacock's shreik and said 'Why, James, what can have happened? Just look at Burton! How can I send him home to his Mother like that? Glory Sakes!' And she took Burton upstairs to get a cold compression on his eye. James sat on at the table and wouldn't speak, not even to Georgina when she said 'Attaboy, James. Up the Old World!'

He was still sitting there when Uncle George came in

looking very serious. 'Who taught you to box, son?' he said and James snapped 'My Father.' 'Well, it was a nice clean tackle,' said Uncle George, 'and he'd have made two of you. Still, he was a guest of the house. Why did you do it?' But James wouldn't answer. However, Uncle George is a very understanding man so he said he supposed James had a good reason but that next time James felt like punching somebody he'd better go to a gymnasium and do it to a ball. After that James went upstairs still saying nothing and Georgina told Uncle George why he had punched Burton. 'Oh, HO! I SEE.' said Uncle George and he did not seem at all angry.

When I went up to bed I heard James thumping his pillow and saying 'Sissy!' in a raging voice so I decided not to say goodnight to him. He is always better if you leave him alone with his rage. But what am I going to do if he goes about punching people? He only seems fierce on the outside because he is so easily hurt inside. Mother and I know that. But do *they*, I wonder. Oh, dear, boys are very difficult to rear.

... September

I knew it. I knew it would happen after yesterday. James has been having a Bilious Attack and Aunt Harriet and Georgina and I have been looking after him. Men have to be looked after so much more than women when they are ill. I sat reading beside him this afternoon while he was asleep. And then it turned out that he wasn't asleep after all but making up a poem. 'Write it down quickly, Sabrina,' he said, 'or it will go out of my head.' So I have put it in my Dairy and here it is.

I remember the yellow Fields,
But once they were green;
I remember the Badger's hole by the river
And going with Albert
To stop up the Foxes Earths before hunting.
I remember the Blackbird's nest in the Ivy
And how funny it is, my children,
That a Blackbird, which is a black bird,
Should have greenish blue eggs
With brown spots
And that a Thrush, which is a brown bird,
Should have greenish blue eggs
With black spots,
That is how you tell them.
I remember the time I was lost in Hareholt
And the time I had my tonsils out
And went to sleep with a smell
That was like the sound of drums drumming
And woke up and had calves-foot jelly

And a sore throat.
I remember the Cowslip Field
By Turk's Farm
And the day we found the wounded Snipe
Up by Gill Hope.
I remember Mrs Leeves' home-made ginger-ale
And helping Jim dig the Mangolds
In the Bottom Meadow.
I remember the Hop Fields
Like dark green tunnels
And stamping the hops into the pig-bags
To make them tighter.
I remember the Gypsy singing
'Ero, the lovely man
That went to Galway riding a drake',
And the Rat Hole under the bread oven
And the place where the Hen Pheasant built her nest
Close to the nut hedge
With seventeen young ones.
I remember everything,
There is nothing I do not remember
Ever since I was born
And even before.

And after that he felt better.

*

. . . September

Today has been Sunday, very still and sunny like Sunday at Thornfield but we did not have to go to Church, thank Goodness. After lunch we felt we had eaten too much which is what Sunday does to you everywhere. So we sat under the big green umbrella in the garden and the house seemed to be quivering in the sunlight, like air over a bonfire. Uncle George's house is white with green shutters. It is larger and not so straggly as Thornfield. It has no name but is just called after Uncle George. A white board at the gate says 'George W. Seaton' and that's all. Of course, this way is very proud and noble but it is difficult to get to know a house unless it has a name. It is like meeting somebody at a party and not knowing what to call them. The woods come right up to the house and all day long the crickets whistle in the trees. When we felt better from lunch we went into the woods and they folded over us and suddenly for the first time I could smell America. The scent came right up out of the earth, very sunny and dry, the kind of scent that makes your nose crinkle up deliciouslly. You only begin to know a place or a person when you can smell them.

We walked very carefully because trees do not hold their breath so much if they can't hear you coming, and we found an old log and sat down on it and James said 'Guess what I can see when I shut my eyes? Mr Oliphant with his trousers very tight and his hair very loose riding down Pound Hill on his Bicycle.' So I shut my eyes, too, and I could see the River Rother and Miss Pidgeon walking over Pound Bridge. And the smoke curling up from Froghole which is a farm built entirely from old ships. And the oak grove which is the result of Admiral Collingwood. He never went out walking without dropping acorns out of his pocket so that there would always be oaks for English ships. I could see Mother in her room doing her hair with her arms bent upwards like the handles of Father's rowing cups. But I could not see him because he is in the R.A.F. and I do not know what that looks like.

But then I said we had better stop trying to see things in our heads because after all what is the Good. You might as well open your eyes and really look. So we did that and presently found a very lucky thing, a huge green catterpillar three inches long with a horn on its nose which we decided to keep till it turned into a moth.

Then somebody called from the house and we came out of the woods to find Uncle George sitting on the porch with an old lady whose face was so wrinkled that it looked like the map of the world. Uncle George said 'This is my Great-aunt Porter.' You would have thought Uncle George a bit too old for a Great-aunt, but No. Aunt Porter did not ask us about our names and ages or even if we had seen bombs. She just said 'Hump!' in a sweet chirpy voice and looked at us without blinking, just like a bird. Then she said suddenly, like something jumping out of a box, 'What is the most wonderful thing you ever saw in your life?'

'Glory sakes!' said James. Then he thought for a minute and said 'Saffron's calf.'

Aunt Porter tossed her head and said 'Pooh, only a calf? That's Nothing.'

'It is so something.' said James. 'I saw it the very moment it was born because I was helping Jim Leeves pull it out with a rope. It was chestnut with a white star on its nose and very sticky.'

'O well,' said Aunt Porter rather unwillingly 'I suppose that's something. But I'm sure Sabrina can do better than a calf!'

So I thought and I agreed with myself that my most wonderful thing was the Christmas Rose. Mother and Albert tried to grow them for ages but at last they gave up and forgot all about them. Then last year when the snow was on the ground and the pipes had burst and we were cooking with ice from the river Mother came in and said 'Guess.' We all guessed but nobody was right. So she took her hand from behind her back and there was a Christmas Rose standing up on its round stem with the dark green leaf and the little flush of pink under the white petals. It was like a Prince. Even Flora and Annie said O, and when Albert saw it he could hardly speak for rage, because it turned out that it had come from Mother's clump and not his. I told Aunt

Porter about it and she said 'H'm yes. Not bad, not bad. But now let me tell you mine.' And I could see she had only asked us so that she could have an excuse to tell *her* wonderful thing, which is something you can understand very well.

'The most wonderful and interesting thing I ever saw' she said, 'was the planet Saturn through a Telescope. He has seven rings round him all made of stars and I've seen them all. Think of that!' And she looked at us triumphantly as though she had created the Planet Saturn herself.

'Also,' she said, 'I once knew a man who told me there were all sorts of rare and unnamed birds in New Giunea and he said if I gave him the money he would go there and call one after me. Wouldn't that have been splendid? A green and yellow one with a long red tail. The Porter Bird, wonderful!'

'And did he?' said James. And Aunt Porter said 'Alas, no, poor man, I couldn't spare the money for his fare.'

Then she said she supposed we would soon be going to school and Uncle George said 'Of course.' But at that Aunt Porter looked very fierce and said 'Of course, nothing. There is far too much education.'

'I know, I know,' said Uncle George hurriedly, 'You have often told me so.'

'And some day you will realise how right I am.' said Aunt Porter. Then she told him that the only things really necessary for education were Singing and Dancing and a

Thorough Knowledge of the Stars in Their Courses. 'And,' she added, 'a few good Speeches like Four Score Years Ago.'

I asked her what Four Score Years Ago was because it sounded like the beginning of a story and Uncle George said hurriedly 'Now, don't bother Aunt Porter.'

'You mean to say you don't know Four Score Years Ago?' said Aunt Porter. 'How very shocking. I will say it for you.'

Uncle George gave a moan and she said 'Surely, George you would not like James or Sabrina to grow up into half-educated, undernourished Ignoramuses, would you? Listen!'

Then Aunt Porter recited the speech. It is by a man called Abraham Lincoln and I have copied it from a book in Uncle George's study to write down here.

'Four Score and Seven years Ago our Fathers brought forth on this Continent a new nation conceived in Liberty and dedicated to the proposition that all men are created equal.

Now we are engaged in a great civil war, testing whether that nation, or any nation so conceived and so dedicated, can long endure. We are met on the great battlefield of that war. We have come to dedicate a portion of that field as a final resting-place for those who here gave their lives that that nation might live. It is altogether fitting and proper that we should do this.

But in a larger sense, we cannot dedicate, we cannot

consecrate, we cannot hallow, this ground. The brave men, living and dead, who struggled here have consecrated it far above our poor power to add or detract. The world will little note nor long remember what we say here but it can never forget what they did here. It is for us, the living, rather, to be dedicated here to the unfinished work which they who fought here have thus far so nobly advanced. It is rather for us to be here dedicated to the great task remaining for us – that from these honoured dead we take increased devotion to that cause for which they gave the last full measure of devotion; that we here highly resolve that these dead shall not have died in vain; that this nation, under God, shall have a new birth of freedom; and that government of the people, by the people, for the people, shall not perish from the earth.'

I could not understand all the speech but while Aunt Porter was saying it I could feel it humming inside me like the rolling of drums and marching feet and when she came to the end she was silent for a minute. Then she said 'For us, the living. That speech goes for England, too, my children.' and got up to go. She has thin pretty feet and she walks on them proudly as though they had springs in them. She walked away and got into her car without taking any more notice of anybody. You had the feeling that she was living her own life and not a bit interested in anybody else's. And that is a comforting thing. I like Aunt Porter. She is a little like Aunt Christina but not so fierce. Also she gives you the feeling that she knows many wonderful secrets and may tell you one of them at any moment.

... September

One of the best parts of today really happened last night. When we looked out of the window there were little lights, silver and gold, dancing through the air and we knew they must be fireflies. James said 'O, they make my mouth water, they are just like our glow-worms, only winged.' And early this morning he made up a quick poem and shouted to me to write it down.

'Watch me,' said the Firefly
'Shine in the dark blue air,'
'Pooh,' said the Glow-worm,
'I can shine anywhere!'

'I'm brighter than you,' said the Firefly
'My light is far more rare.'
But the glow-worm lifted his candle-tail
And said 'I don't care,
Nothing you say makes any difference
So there!'

Aunt Harriet's plan for today was that we were to go to tea with Mrs Mayday next door. We have been wanting to do that ever since we came because Patrick says there are two Woodchucks in Mrs Mayday's wood. Her house is just like Uncle George's except that it has blue shutters. Mrs Mayday has a baby inside her that is going to be born very soon. That is why she is so peaceful. She has dark eyes that seem to look through you and a slow dark voice that says 'S-a-b-r-i-n-a D-e-a-r' in a long drawl that makes you feel warm and delicious. That is because she comes from the South, Patrick says, which is a part of America where nearly all the people are black and speak with drawls.

Mr Mayday is a Business Man and quite young. Practically all American men are business men. Micky says that is why they die young. Because when they stop doing business they don't know how to do anything else and are At a Loss and death is the only thing. This seems a great Pity for their wives. There are two large cemeteries near here. They are very neat and clean with American flags stuck in some of the graves and many very small houses. I think these must contain business men. I hope Uncle George will not give up Oil for a very long time.

Mr and Mrs Mayday took us into their wood and one of the woodchucks, which they call Gracie, leapt across the path just in front of us. She was a little like a cat and a little like a rabbit but larger than either. Gracie is our first real American animal.

There are Dog Kennels in the woods, too, and nineteen dogs of a special kind used in the Belgian army. They carry water and bandages and brandy round their necks to wounded soldiers on the Battlefield. Sometimes the dogs will take messages from soldiers saying where they are wounded. If it is in the leg somebody comes back with the dog and a stretcher and all ends well and the soldier is saved. Mr Mayday keeps on breeding these dogs though it seems rather useless now that there is no Belgian army any more.

Mrs Mayday showed us where to find four different kinds of Michaelmas Daisy which are called Astors here and Sweet-scented-mellilot and Hickory Nuts and a nest of Large Black Beetles. And once she put her hand up to a branch and said 'O!' very softly and there hanging on the underside was a beautiful pale green moth, soft and dusty, the largest moth we had ever seen. 'That's an I-m-p-e-r-i-a-l.' said Mrs Mayday and we all stood gazing at it. Mrs Mayday reminds me a little bit of Pel. They both know the names of flowers and the things you find in woods and they both love them. Also neither of them ask you any questions but just live their own lives. And that makes it easier to tell them about yours. Whenever I think of either of them I remember the Vixen I once saw at the edge of Ratt's Clearing, dancing by herself in the sunshine. And Saunders said 'Wummen and vixens, they be two of a kind, dancing alone with their secrets.'

Mrs Mayday had made a Treat for us, real English tea with muffins and strawberries-and-cream. Mr Mayday says you can get strawberries-and-cream in America all the year round instead of only in June – think of that! You can't wonder the Americans are proud of their country. And after tea we went upstairs to see the Nursery. Mrs Mayday walks forward just as if she were going backwards. That is because of the baby inside her. James and I thought it must be a very small one or else curled up very tightly. But she said No, not now. That now it is like a swimmer getting ready to dive and soon it will dive headfirst into the world and she hopes it will be a boy. I hope so, too, because I think I like boys best though they are harder to rear.

The little clothes are very small and beautiful. I wish I had a baby inside me.

... September

Today Aunt Harriet had a Bridge Party which is a great number of people playing cards the whole time, which must be very dull. So she sent us in the car with Micky to see Jason, Jane and Mirabel Campbell, the friends of our childhood. They are staying at a place called New Canaan. It has nothing to do with Palestine or the Promised Land as you might think. On the way Micky stopped the car outside a place called Rumpley's Bar and said 'I've a throat on me like a Cross-cut Saw. Will yez come in and have a Coke while I refashion meself with a thumbler of Beer?'

At first we thought we had better not but Micky said that anybody can go into a Bar in America. Even a Babe Newborn. So we went in and sat at a long counter behind which were a great number of beautiful coloured bottles. It was just like the Bar at the End House, the Village Inn at Thornfield, which was built by Queen Elizabeth for one of her favourite Chancellors. But in England you are not allowed inside a Bar until you are sixteen. When the others go in for drinks and dart games we have to wait outside the door and our noses get red in winter. But sometimes for a treat Mr Feyning, who keeps the Inn, asks us into his private sitting-room for a Cordial Drink and from there you can peer into the Bar until somebody notices you and reminds you that you're only eleven. It is awful to be young. You are not allowed to stay up late and you must always be washing and you never have enough money and you can't go into a Bar.

All our best friends meet at the End House. Mr Tanner, United Dairy, Mr Rayne, the Taxi, Mr Naylor the Barber and Roly Higgins who makes coffins and is cross-eyed so you are never sure if he is looking at you or someone else. They are always laughing and teasing each other and discussing the News and Mr Churchill and Invasion. Once when we were looking in unobserved I heard Pel remark that she had been target-practising with the pistol Father had given her. Mr Tanner said 'O-HO' and Mr Rayne said 'A-HA' and Roly Higgins said 'So *that's* how Ed Potter got hit in the head and not expected to recover.' And they all looked solemn and shocked. We knew it was a joke because of the way they said it but soon everybody, including Father and Mother, were pitying Old Ed and wondering if he would last the night. They went on so long that at last Pel was convinced she *had* killed Ed Potter though she was shooting in the opposite direction and on the way home she wanted to call in at Hawkesden just to make sure. But Father said 'You've done enough damage. Let the old man die in peace!' And then we giggled and Pel realised it was only a joke. But the funny part of it was that the next day an iron hook fell from the roof on to Ed's head and he had to wear a bandage and everybody teased her so much that she could only get the blue ring on the target and never the Bull's Eye ever afterwards.

Well, we had two coke's each and after a while Micky's throat was cured so we went on to the Campbells. They have quite settled down in America with their Mother and say they can hardly tell it from England now. Jason goes to an American public school which is not the same as an English one but a place where you pay nothing and get everything which is very generous. Jane goes to the same kind of school only higher. She is rather worried about her education because she says everything is much too easy and she does not have any Latin even though she is nearly twelve. Perhaps that means James will not have Latin either. I will be glad of that because he won't be going around shouting Quis and Ego and Nil Desperandum and Agricola a Farmer in his old superior way. Mirabel has a scholarship and that entitles you to go to a grand school for nothing which is a relief to anybody who can only bring ten pounds away from England.

We all sat in the sun outside their house talking about England and America. Mirabel said 'Do you remember the ferretting at Gill Hope and the time we damned up the River to make a bathing pool and nearly drowned James?' 'Yes,' said Jane. 'And how we used to go with Saunders and his dog Flannel to feed the Pheasants and his son Pecky whistling them through the woods with his high curlew whistle. Ooh, it made your backbone shiver.'

'Yes, and finding the sky-lark's nest in the Hill Meadow and Jason saying "Always round, always round. Are there no square nests?" And Saunders saying that God never made anything square. All corners? He wouldn't be so stoopid.'

'Yes and nightingales keeping you awake at night till somebody throws a boot at them.'

Jane said 'When we go back we shall be remembering things about America just this way.'

And James said 'Yes. We've got two countries now.' And we all felt rich and prosperous and important. It is not everybody who has two countries to belong to.

On the way home Micky asked us if we had ever been to Ireland. He said 'Tell me about it, then, so I can cheer meself up by feeling homesick.' So we told him all we could remember, specially about going fishing in the curraghs and riding horses along the strand.

'Isn't it a queer thing,' he said, 'that in the whole state of New York you'd hardly find enough horses to make a small race meeting. How they can live without a horse has me beat.'

We said they seemed to live very well and happily without horses. The more you argue with a really Irish person the more they will talk so we argued with Micky. And he got very wild and waved one hand and drove with the other. 'Look at that!' he shouted and we looked at the woods that were running by the road. 'Divil a plant at all or the seed of a cauliflower. Not even a cabbage in the whole stretch of it.' And we said why should there be cabbages, America has California for a vegetable garden and does not need to spoil the woods.

'Well then,' said Micky, 'if you put these fields down in Ireland they'd be tilled so fine you could grow angels in every inch of them. Ireland's the gem of the world.' Then James asked him if he thought that way why did he come to America. And Micky looked at him ferociously and waved both hands and roared 'Why is it? It's the way I'd be having only one leg to me pants and me belly pressed against me backbone with the emptiness in it. And six children after meself in historical succession. It was that way. And when I found it was a country devoid of horses I took to motor cars which have been me pride and care ever since. America's the gem of the world, God save it.'

The interesting thing about Micky is that whenever you think he is in a particular place with one idea he is always somewhere else with another. When we got home he said we could polish the car and went to sleep and snored with the sunset on his face.

When Aunt Harriet came out she gave one look at him and said 'Did he stop at Rumpley's?' And when we said yes she said 'Tch, tch tch, that accounts for it.' Then she smiled her crinkly smile and said 'Come in to supper, my lambs.'

. . . September
Every morning Aunt Harriet comes in and wakes us saying

'Let us then be up and Doing
With a heart for any Fate.'

She says that is the American Way of Life and it was invented by Longfellow. You cannot afford to be lazy in America or you would wake up to find you had missed something.

Today I had a great shock. Georgina told me it would not be long now before we were moving on and when she said that my heart seemed to fall into my stomach. Because what was going to happen to us next and what would we do without Aunt Harriet and Uncle George?

'I don't mean you're leaving *us*, silly!' said Georgina. 'We'll *all* be moving on. In the winter holidays we shall probably be going to Florida.' Oh, what a relief! I am glad there is still some time till Winter because we have hardly got used to being here yet and cannot even think about moving on. Georgina then told me that we will go to Maine in the Summer and snow places for ski-ing when it is cold and also to Bermuda where you go out in a boat and catch sharks if they do not catch you. When I asked her how we were going to get educated with so much else to do she said 'Oh, in between times, unfortunately.'

Of course, that will be lovely for James who always wants to be some place where he isn't. But I like to stay still in one place for a long time like a plant coming up every year. In Grandfather's garden he has planted the names of all his treasured people in crocuses. They come up every Spring like the Resurrection of the Dead. Gran is there and

Mother and Father and James and me and Pel and Martin and Madge and Cousin Fiona who is so old she remembers Queen Victoria as a girl. Tarquin, our brother is there, too, who died before I was born and Aunt Christina but not Aunt Betsy because Grandfather cannot abide her. He says 'I won't have that woman turning the other cheek in *my* garden if she *is* my sister!' She bores him because she does so many good works without enjoying them and is always telling how her hair caught on Disralei's waistcoat button when she was a little gal. Disralei was a Polititian.

But when I told Georgina about wanting to stay still she said that was no good. She says if I were thirteen I would understand that you have to have things happen to you all the time otherwise you might as well die. Thirteen it seems is a very difficult age because by then you have stopped being a child and haven't yet turned into a grown-up. 'Life seems to be running past you and you can't catch it,' she said 'and you feel happy one day and miserable the next and like people and don't like them all in one breath and Nobody Understands You.' And when she said it she looked quite young, almost as young as James.

'Come into my room,' she said 'and I'll show you a secret.' The secret was a little box full of small pieces of paper folded up. 'Those are my Beaux.' said Georgina. Beaux is American for the boys you like and sometimes if your Mother is in a good mood you can go to the Movies with them if other people are going too. To play this secret you put the names of thirty-two of the Beaux into the box and every night take out one and throw it away without looking at it. On the last day of the month there is one left and you look at it and that is the one you are going to marry.

I said whichever way you did it, it must come out differently each time and she said 'Of course it does, silly.' 'But,' I said, 'you can't marry one every month can you?' And she said she thought English kids were pretty dumb.

Then she gave me a box for Beaux but I do not know thirty-two boys. I could only think of William and Walter and James and Jason and Matthew, So I put in Uncle George and Martin and Step-Uncle Cedric who was a Neer-do-well and went to India and married a black lady and we have some black step-cousins, and Mr Oliphant in spite of his beard and of course the First Officer on the boat and Pecky Saunders and Mr Churchill and the President of the United States. But Georgina got frightfully cross when she saw the names and said I was not being serious and took the box back. I didn't mind because I don't really want to marry anybody just yet though I would like to be a Mother. I don't think Georgina does either because after a while she said it was a silly game and she only did it to keep up with her friends, Barbara and Caroline-Ann. 'If you don't go with the Gang you get left out and feel lonely.' she said. 'But you're only a child, Sabrina, you wouldn't understand.'

And just at that moment Aunt Harriet came in and said 'Glory sakes! Sitting indoors on such a beautiful day! Why, don't you know that Childhood is the Best Time of your Lives and you must make the fullest use of it. Run along out now and play tennis or go for a ride. Do *something* anyway.' And Georgina gave a loud groan and went thumping down the stairs.

We found James in the stables so we saddled the horses and Georgina switched off the current of the fence before we set out. This fence is an electric one. It consists of one wire strung on poles and the moment cattle try to get past it they are surprised and electrified. It is a much simpler way than waiting years for a thorn hedge to grow. Everything is done the quickest way in America and no time is wasted.

Down by the lake there were wild grapes, like the ones Leaf Erickson found, I suppose, and when I got down to pick some Georgina shrieked 'Look out!' And there was a long creeper coming right round my legs. It was Poison Ivy. This is a very common American plant which gives you pimples and nothing can cure them except a special ointment. We stepped carefully past it and ate great bunches of grapes and after that we bathed under a sign that said No Swimming Allowed. It was cold and draughty in the water but very dilecious and I felt that I was really right inside America. We dried in the sun afterwards and James found some very small wild sunflowers and white everlastings and made wreaths for all of us. Then we just tied our clothes round our waists and rode home feeling very fresh and triumphant.

'Hello, savages!' said Aunt Harriet. She was standing in the doorway and her face looked like Faith Hope Charity but the greatest is Charity as Moses said. She had a newspaper in her hand and she said 'Listen, I've got a lovely plan for Tomorrow. What about the World's Fair?' And suddenly I knew why she looked so gentle and was making tomorrow's plan today. I looked at the newspaper and it said in black letters 'German Bombs Take Heavy Toll of London and South East England.' It was like being hit very hard in the stomach. James said 'Sabrina, I am going to be sick.' So I gave him my last bit of chewing-gum and he chewed it and felt better. 'It's all right, Lambs, it's all right. We'd have heard if anything had happened.' said Aunt Harriet in her soothing voice. 'Go up now and change and after Supper we will play Rummy.'

We did that and Uncle George made funny faces and jokes and Georgina was very friendly and Aunt Harriet kept making the most promising plans so we kept our minds off the newspaper till we went to bed.

When you are in bed you are safe. Nothing can hurt you. And a good way to stop thinking is to go round the world in your head. Vesuvius all in flames and South Africa where Uncle Cedric captured the Gorilla and Brazil where coffee grows on trees and China where they keep eggs a hundred years and the cities are forbidden. And India full of Untutored Millions and Iceland and the Polar Wastes and the Islands of the Equator. Round and round you go and if you are very careful you do not get to the one important place till you are asleep. Then it doesn't matter. But sometimes you slip off the track and there you are in England and you cannot pretend any more and your heart aches.

... *September*

It is much easier to go round the world in your head than at the World's Fair, it doesn't hurt your feet so much. The first country we met when we got out of the Greyhound Bus was Italy, a lady with a huge green waterfall flowing out of her down to a little lake. But Aunt Harriet said we had better go to Great Britain first. Great Britain has no waterfall but it has a large hall in the middle of which is a sort of four-poster bed and there is Magna Charta. This is an unreadable paper signed by King John at the point of the Barons' swords to make us all free. In Great Britain you can see all the British Industries and stamp collections and coats-of-arms and in one special room there were bombs and shells and guns and bullets and parachutes all laid out very neatly. The most beautiful thing of all was a brass ship's proppellor which looked like a large gold clover leaf. When we had seen everything we went to the Newsreel which showed German bombs being dropped on Dover Harbour. And every one of them missed. If they go on doing that all will be well.

Everything in the World's Fair is very large. You look at the feet of a statue and have to tilt your head back to see the rest. The statues are usually of Freedom or statesmen but there is one woman riding a horse in a Frenzy. One of the nicest things in the Fair is the Borden Dairy which has a revolving stage full of performing cows. You see them being milked by Mechanical Milkers into glass tubes. Jim Leeves says cows are the most private and sensitive animals but perhaps in America they do not mind going on the stage. Or else they have got used to it.

The next thing we saw was the man-made lightning which the pamphlet says is going to be very useful for the Future. James asked Aunt Harriet if we might be going to run out of the supply of God's lightning. She said No, but that scientists had always to be thinking of the Future because you never know. Some of it was yellow like ordinary lightning but the rest was pink and blue and very beautiful and each time it made a humming, crackling noise like a humming top, the sound you think of when you think of the world turning. Aunt Harriet liked the Man-made lightning because it gave her a chance to sit down.

After that we chose the American City Old and New.

The old part was a dark little cobbled street, nearly as dangerous as the London blackout. There were ladies in long hair sitting by the little windows and old-fashioned clothes and wigs, and a little old theatre and the sound of horses slowly clopping along the cobble-stones. This is what New York must have looked like long ago. Then suddenly the street turned a corner and became very modern, much bigger and better but not nearly so exciting, and at the end of it there is a mountain of lit-up tin which gets larger and smaller while an organ plays. This is done in praise of Electric Light, a Boon and a Blessing to men.

After that, luckily, it was time for lunch. We could look out at the pavilions while we were eating. They all have strange and beautiful shapes. One of them is built like the bow of a ship and another has an enormous powder-box on top, enough to last you a lifetime. And one is made entirely of a waterfall. 'Is Niagara bigger than this?' said James and Aunt Harriet sighed and said 'Yes, James.'

The next thing after luncheon was the Mechanical Man and his Dog. He talked and smoked a cigarette when the button was pressed. James wanted to know if he was the Man of the Future and Aunt Harriet said Quite Possibly. 'But,' said James, 'wouldn't it be awful if you had to wait for somebody to press a button before you could move or speak.' But Aunt Harriet thought it might be restful in a way, especially when it came to asking questions. She was getting rather tired.

Alongside the Mechanical Man was the Time Capsule which is not the ordinary kind you take medicine in but a large one made of bronze with a glass window in the front. You look down through a hole and see it hundreds of feet down in the earth. In it are papers and buttons and razors and a lady's hat and a faded doll and a Bible and a camera and seeds and cotton wool, etc, and a notice saying 'Do Not Open for Five Thousand Years.' The idea is that somebody will dig up the capsule some day and find out all about the American culture of today. But what if there is nobody left in five thousand years? It is a long time. The Time Capsule is another thing about the Future.

The next thing was the Theme Centre. This is a large ball standing beside a large dagger. They are called Perisphere and Trylon. You go up a moving staircase into the ball and solemn music is played and a man speaks from the ceiling and you look down upon the country of the Future. This is a very clean place with houses and churches and aerodromes and bathing-pools and schools and amusement parks and all of them model. 'Will there also be model people?' said James and Aunt Harriet said she hoped so. As it grew lighter we saw that the woods and lakes and fields were very model also. Neat and well swept with no animals except model squirrels and a few model rabbits. 'What about the lions and tigers and eagles of the future?' said James. 'They will be in a Zoo.' said Aunt Harriet. 'And now, let us go to the Clock Work Trains. They simply mustn't be missed.'

So we went to the Railroads Secton where there was a panorama (scenery) of towns and wharves and ferries and mountains and tunnels and bridges. One man pressed a button and another spoke from the ceiling telling us that we were about to see the Railways of Tomorrow. Then several little trains began to run along tracks by the stations and through the tunnels and over bridges. There was even a little finicular (mountain train) running up the mountains. The trains went backwards and forwards shunting and load-ing and steaming and changing engines and Aunt Harriet kept saying 'Look! O Look!' in a high excited voice. The noise of the trains was a steady buzz and the voice of the man was a steady hum and presently James and I must have dozed off. I woke with a jerk when I heard Aunt Harriet gave a little shriek of surprise and say in an outraged voice 'Well, really, you are the most Extroadinary Pair! I never met a child who would go to sleep over Clockwork Trains. Why, I came here simply to please you!'

'Well,' said James, '*we* came here simply to please *you*!'

'Me!' said Aunt Harriet. 'Why, Glory Sakes, James, I simply detest clockwork trains.'

'So do we!' said James and we all burst out laughing and Aunt Harriet said if we'd only told her before she would have taken the opportunity to go to sleep herself.

Well, that was over so the next thing we chose was the Futurama which is a display of the future by that part of the world known as General Motors. We had forty minutes to wait in the cue so we kept asking Aunt Harriet riddles to take her mind off it because she is not as young as she was. But very soon she asked us not to bother as it would be more soothing for her to be Quite Quiet. Well, at last we got in. In the darkness the music poured over us and a row of moving chairs came up out of the floor and we each got in one and were carried away. A man's voice said just behind me 'Man has forged ahead since 1940' but when I looked round there was nothing there but the back of the seat. Then we were carried into a little tunnel and could look through a glass window at some more of the Future with fields and woods made of different coloured pieces of worn velvet and churches and orchards and farms and villages and cities. Some of the orchards had little umbrellas of glass over them, to keep out the frost and Whenever we passed anything like this the voice at the back said 'Strange? Fantastic? Unbelievable? Remember this is the world of 1960.' But no matter how quickly you turned round there was never anybody there.

In the middle of the Futurama there were roads full of

motor-cars the size of small beetles. Some were going slowly and some quickly and some quicker still but all of them going. The roads went over everything, river and dams and reservoirs and rocky mountains and the cars kept moving along them. You simply couldn't escape. No matter how difficult the deserts and crevasses were the road always got there in the end and the motor cars got there with it. Then the voice said '1940 is twenty years ago, All Eyes to the Future!' but just as I was looking round for it another man pulled me off my chair and the seats moved on and we came out into the air.

'Will England be like that in 1960?' said James but Aunt Harriet thought that England being so old-fashioned a place would not catch up to the Futurama till about Two thousand and Twenty. 'Well, I shall be nearly eighty-nine then,' said James 'and probably too old to mind. Still, it will be nice to have central heating in the orchard at Thornfield.'

It is funny how hard it is to imagine the future. You try and it is like a dark curtain. Every time you move towards it you move in little jumps, like the hops of a Robin. And then the curtain moves away a little further. It never goes up, just moves back another step.

James said 'What about us going to something that is not the future but Right Now.'

Aunt Harriet said there wasn't such a thing at the Fair but we reminded her of the Amusement Park and she gave a little groan and said 'Lovely!' We were very careful of her on the way there in case her feet should give out.

First we went on the Ferris Wheel and the Swinging Boats and the Aeroplanes while Aunt Harriet sat on a seat and bowed her head. Then a man dressed like the Lone Star Ranger took us on the Parachute Jump and we saw the whole Fair spread out below us before we came down with a whizzing jerk that breaks your fall at the bottom. Then James wanted to go and see the Premature Babies. Aunt Harriet raised her head and said 'No, no!' but he insisted and said he still had twenty-five cents and Aunt Harriet was not vital enough to argue. When he came back he said the man in charge had told him all the babies had been born before their time and asked Aunt Harriet what *was* their time. But Aunt Harriet just moaned and said she would die if he asked her one more question.

By that time we had only twenty cents left and those were mine so we went on the Merry-go-round which was the best way of enjoying Now that we could think of. The funny thing about a Merry-go-round is that the faster it moves the stiller it seems to become. It is not you but the outside world that is turning. We rode horses called Marcus and Mayflower and the music grew louder and the World's Fair went spinning round us. Whenever I go on a merry-go-round I seem to be riding home, not to Thornfield but to some place that reminds me of Thornfield but is deeper

inside the world. It is a funny feeling, sad and happy at the same time.

That was the last thing of the World's Fair. As we went away we could hear the music faintly and the lights began to gleam in the darkness. Micky met us at the gate and said to Aunt Harriet 'Are ye destroyed entirely?' and she said in a fainting voice 'Don't speak of it!' She went to sleep on the way home and we made her a pillow of our coats and sat still and talked in careful whispers just like model people out of the World of the Future.

. . . September

Today Aunt Harriet was in a State of Exhuastion and could not get up. So we went to her room and there she was sitting up in bed with a black bandage under her chin to prevent a double one and waving some letters in her hand.

Uncle George said 'English Mail!' and I could hardly speak when I saw the writing. There was one for James from Father and one from Mother to me. 'Aren't you going to open them?' said Aunt Harriet so I slit mine open. 'Are they well?' said Uncle George. And I said Yes though I had not read any of it. Then he said suddenly 'I know. Perhaps you would like to go away and read them alone?' Uncle George is a very understanding man.

So we went to my room and read both letters several

times. And, oh, they are quite well and the bombs have not touched them. Thornfield is safe and Mother and Miss Minnett are still there and Flora and Annie and the dogs and Mouse and the horses. Albert has been called up. One of the ponies has foaled, a filly. Mr Oliphant has influenza but not badly. Mr Tanner and Mr Rayne are now Parashots and keep watch with Mr Feyning and Roly Higgins on the Church Tower. The apples are being stored and the herbs dried and the pickles made.

Mother said 'Be sure to wear your blue coat in the cold weather and warn James to remember to change his pants. You know what he's like.' She said everybody had asked after us, Miss Pidgeon and Mr Feyning and Jim Leeves and Mrs Gadd. I could see them all, stopping her in the lanes or the Village and asking her and she answering with her little doe-like smile.

Father told James all about the R.A.F. and how he is now in the Ground Command as he is a bit too old to go into the air, which is a relief. But Martin is in the Flying Arm and is bringing down enough Germans for the two of them. He said 'I like to think of you both having such a good time in America. Tell Aunt Harriet she is a Glorious Woman.'

So we went in and told her that and she was very pleased and said 'Dear John!' Then she said 'Lambs, what *will* you do? I've no plan for today!' But we told her that was quite a relief in a way because yesterday's was such a big one.

And James said she must stay in bed all day because, after all, it was our fault she was exhuasted and that tonight he would take his gun and a rug and sleep out in the shrubbery near the garage. 'To protect you from harm.' he said. And she thought that was a good idea.

So James and I just maendered about in the garden, smelling things and thinking of the letters. I had mine tucked into my knickers and I kept feeling it to make sure it was there. Later on Mrs Mayday came through the wood and in her hands she had a chipmunk, which is a sort of small golden squirrel with black stripes and we brought him in and gave him peanuts out of Uncle George's cocktail cabinet. The baby is getting very heavy now to carry around and Mrs Mayday keeps her arms folded over it. She said 'S-a-b-r-i-n-a is a l-o-v-e-l-y name, just like a r-i-v-e-r.' And James said 'Well, that is not strange because it *is* a river.' Then Mrs Mayday said 'Listen!' And we listened and James said 'I hear a cat. Is it a wild cat?' She shook her head and pointed and whispered 'A catbird!' And a greyish black bird came hopping along a branch, weighing it down, and giving little miaowing cries just like a cat. Then it flew away through the wood still mewing and Mrs Mayday followed it.

It was a quiet sort of day. We could feel America running through us very comfortingly and every now and then I felt the elastic to see if my letter was there and it always was. In the evening Uncle George let us sit in his study and told us about the Time When he was a Boy and we told him how anxious we were that he should not give up business and die and he said he would try not to.

After that it was time for James to go and protect Aunt Harriet so he took a rug and went out with his gun and we all went to bed early. But it was simply no time before there was frightful shouting and James came rushing through the front door yelling 'Help, help!' Aunt Harriet and Uncle George rushed down in their dressing-gowns and James shouted 'Who put out all the lights? I am not a bit afraid of sleeping all by myself in the shrubbery even if there *are* Burglars behind the lilac. But why are the lights out?' I knew he was frightened though he would not admit it.

Aunt Harriet explained that the lights always went out when the household went to bed. Then she suggested that he should sleep in the drawing-room tonight instead of the shrubbery, 'Begin in a small way and work up.' she said. So after a little persuading he said he would as he could probably protect her better if he were a little nearer. So he is sleeping down there now with his gun and his blanket. And I am up here writing. The stars are shining tonight and I have wished. They are very far and small but that is because they are faithfully watching over England as well.

*

Today has been very rememorable. Directly after breakfast when Aunt Harriet was on the point of making a plan for the day we heard a frightful noise outside just like kettles and old iron rattling together and guns going off. Nelly dropped a pile of plates and shreiked and the rest of us ran to the door in terror. And what do you think it was? Pel. She ran up the steps dropping her gloves and kissed us all and it turned out that she'd come to take James and me for a day in New York. We rushed for our hats and coats and as soon as we got outside we knew what had made the noise. It was a very old car lent her by a friend who told her we must take care of it because though he has several better cars this is his Treasure. 'It's a Mormon!' said Pel. 'You mean a Marmon!' said Aunt Harriet. 'No, I don't.' said Pel. 'Wait till we drive off and you'll see its a Mormon – very vicious.'

Then she did a lot of things with handles and wires and the car began to shiver and the rattling noise began again. Aunt Harriet popped a Dollar into each of our pockets and called out 'Come Back Safely' and presently we were driving along the beautiful highroad all talking together and people hooting and saying 'Hi!' as they passed us. But Pel took no notice. 'Well, how is America?' she said. So we told her all we had been doing and the things we had seen and found and James asked her about the plan for today. She said 'Let's let things just happen. Indeed, when we get to New

York they probably will because I have never driven a car in it before.' But she admitted that there was a sort of Surprise for the afternoon. So we rode along rattling and humming, feeling warm and happy with the trees throwing stripes of light and shadow over us.

At last we came to an enormous bridge and Pel said 'Shut your eyes and don't open them till I tell you.' After a while she said 'Now!' and there below us was a great river all curling silver. On it were steamboats and barges and beyond them in a sunny mist were tall thin buildings standing up in the sky like flames. 'New York!' said Pel. 'Or Babylon!' It was like the places you dream about it, not quite real with the sun over it and the long buildings rising up like fountains. Then we lost them because we were driving through the streets between them. It was like being at the bottom of a river and the blue sky flowing like water overhead.

Presently we stopped at some traffic lights and when they changed to green the car would not move. A fierce man in a blue cap ran towards us blowing a whistle. 'Cop!' whispered Pel and the man said 'Move on, can't you? Don't hold up the traffic. Step on it!' 'Will you tell me what I step on?' said Pel. So he growled and got inside and pulled some handles and when the engine began again he got out very red in the face and said 'You know what you want to do with that car? Burn it.' After that we thought we had better park the

Mormon. We could easily do without it because New York is such an advanced city that you can either go underground or through the air or take a common taxi.

So we decided to go on the air which is the Elevated Railway. This was much noisier than the Mormon and even more exciting. It is a small train like a catterpillar running along the sides of the sides of the houses and you can look in at the windows as you go by and see what everybody is. It must be awful to be so unprivate.

At one place where the train stopped Pel said 'Look! Over there is the tallest building in the world. It is called the Empire State. You can go right to the top.' So we decided to get out and go there and very soon we were going up a lift with our ears crackling. At first when you come out on the top platform you see nothing but sky but when we dared to look over the parapet there was New York spread out beneath us and we were up above all the flaming buildings and the two rivers that wind round them. 'What a sight!' said Pel softly. Then she noticed we were both holding on to her rather tightly. 'Now, take courage and look!' she said. 'This is the very centre of America and the New World swings round it like a wheel. Think, the long white beaches of California and the great Western Mountains and the Southern Seas and the spreading praries, all of them wheeling round this little point where we stand now. Isn't it exciting?' We said it was and we tried to imagine it all and held on to her very tightly. Then we came down in the lift again, plop, like a stone falling.

After this experience we felt we had better have lunch so we ate Hamburgers and Lemon Meringue Pie, which are very American, in a Bar Restaurant and we felt very peaceful sitting there and we told Pel about our letters. She had had some too and she said 'Letters when they begin coming regularly are like the pendulum of a clock, tick-tock, tick-tock, between the countries. After this we shall all know the right time.' The right time, she said, is the time in your heart.

Lunch made us feel light and airy and Pel said we would now go and buy some clothes for Romulus because with all these eggs and butters and sugars in America he is quite growing out of everything. This time we chose to go underground as we had already been in the air. The Subway is not like an English Underground, deep in the Bowels of the Earth, but just underneath the pavement and it makes a fussy clattering old-fashioned sort of noise. Our carriage was full of dark faces. Except for the Porters in Canada they were the first negro people we had seen. I thought they were beautiful. They sat very still and did not fidget with their hands but just gazed out in front of them with dark sleepy eyes. Their faces are full of wonder as though they thought it a surprising and remarkable thing to be alive but were too sleepy to bother about it.

When we came up the steps to the shops Pel said we must be careful not to look at the windows or our mouths would water and what would be the good of that with our Ten Pounds no good any more. But we were no sooner in the shop before she was saying 'O Sabrina what a delicious dress, just your size!' or 'James, do look at the skates!' or 'Gloves, just what I need!' James said 'You can have my dollar!' But she said No, that she didn't *really* want things and it was only people that mattered. So then she kept her eyes averted and only bought what Romulus needed. And while we were shopping little bells rang in the air all the time. Pel says she has never been able to find out why they do it but perhaps it is just a diversion for the shop-assistants.

'And now,' she said, as we came out of the shop, 'let us go and see the Planetarium!'

'Is that the Surprise?' said James but she said No, the surprise came later. James and I had never seen a Planetarium before because there are none in England. At first, if you are late, as we were, you go into a great room where everything is dark and you fall over people's feet and they say Tch, tch, tch. But presently it lightens and there is a ceiling like a great blue dome and on this the stars and constellations come out one by one. All round the lower part of the sky is the outline of New York and the stars march away above it. There you sit watching them and feeling as though you were alone on the top of a Mountain, except for the voice of a hidden man who tells you all about them. They wheel across the sky from evening till morning and the whole night takes only half an hour. Then the lights go up and the stars disappear and you discover the hidden man hiding behind the instrument that made them. After that everybody begins to talk and laugh in the light and the magic is over and you buy a star magazine to remind you of it all.

We came out dazzled with the darkness into a sort of gallery which is filled with enormous black stones full of holes like caves on the seashore. Pel told us that they were dead meteors and I put my hand on one and it felt very cold and ended. We walked all round them imagining them flying through space before they died and suddenly who should we see standing by a meteor much taller than herself but Aunt Porter! She was prodding a large hole with her stick and was not a bit surprised to see us. She just said 'Think of it. Millions of years ago this was a golden spark shooting through the sky, and men said to each other as it went '*Look, a falling star, wish on it!*' Now it is cold. And where are their wishes.'

James said he supposed they were with the people who wished them.

'Hump.' said Aunt Porter. 'But what if they never got them?'

'Well, *somebody* must have got them' said Pel. 'A wish, a proper wish, is a dynamic thing. It is like an arrow from a bow, it must strike somewhere. Somebody gets it, either the wisher or another.' Then Aunt Porter poked at Pel with her stick and said 'Woman, get thee behind me. In another minute I shall be thinking of Heaven and Hell and my immortal soul and the meaning of life.' Pel laughed and said 'Why not? They're the only things worth thinking about.' 'Maybe.' said Aunt Porter. 'But I'm too old for it now. I can only manage meteors. I have no more wishes.' And without another word she walked away on her springy feet and began poking at another one.

'And now,' said Pel, 'I am quite Exhausted so let's have tea.' So we took a common taxi this time through Central Park which is something like Hyde and down Fifth Avenue which is the grand street of New York to a place that was all silver chairs and white mirrors and a man at the door in a silver coat.

Pel looked round and then said quickly 'There they are!' And who do you think it was? Cherry Ripe in a purple coat and a yellow hat and her Uncle Ernie leaning on a stick. They were the Surprise! Cherry shouted 'Ullo!' and we all rushed at each other and everybody talked at once. When we asked Cherry if she was enjoying America she said 'Not Arf!' and it was lovely to find she hadn't changed a bit. She said 'See me new coat? I got two of these, one purple and one green and one of me Ats got a fevver in it, quite small but dynty. Me Uncle Ern's ever such a kind man, so is me

Auntie and they've got a Ford Car. Why, I'm that grand me Mum wouldn't know me.' 'Oh, yes she would' said James. 'All Mothers know their own children. They are like cows, they can smell them.' And Cherry's face stopped dancing for a minute and she said 'I betcher right, Jimes, she would.' Then we asked her if she was allowed to serve in the shop and she said 'Sure. And I elp me Auntie in the Ouse and soon I'm going to school and then on to Igh school and then I'll be trained proper to take care of Mum and the kids at Ome.'

So then we told her all about Aunt Harriet and Uncle George and while we were talking Pel and Uncle Ernie were getting to know each other. It seems that Pel had written to him and asked him to meet us and he was glad to because it turns out that before he was American he came from Yorkshire, which is one of the most English places you can be born in. 'Huddersfield' he said to Pel. 'Came away when I was a lad of sixteen to seek me fortune. I'm American through and through, Yes Mam, and its a fine country. Still you can't change your blood and mine's English and I can tell you that right now its seeing red, Yes Mam.'

And all the time he was talking his brown hair stood up on end and he kept stamping on the ground with his stick. So we told him all we could about England and he told us about America. And he kept on ordering more ices for everybody and told Pel he was sorry he'd never had any children but that Cherry made up to him for everything and he was going to keep her.

'I got to go Ome sometime, Uncle Ern' said Cherry. 'Mum'll be needing me.' And he said 'Well, perhaps someday we'll all go home, kid, on vacation and maybe we'll bring the rest of them back here for a quiet life.'

Isn't that lovely? Think of Cherry's Mum and the kids all coming back to live with Uncle Ernie and serve in the shop and never be poor any more. James said that he wished Uncle Ernie was his uncle and he said at once 'I'd be proud if you'd adopt me, son.' So we adopted him right away and now Cherry and James and I are cousins. Then Uncle Ernie asked for the bill and when Pel wanted to pay it he looked fierce and said 'Mam, get this straight. You're guests in America. And I would like to say here and now that it's a proud pleasure to have you.' So Pel said 'Thank you, Uncle Ernie.' And he laughed because he knew she had adopted him too.

After that we promised to go and see them soon and help Uncle Ernie in the shop and Cherry said 'Be seein you, James, be seeing you, Sabrina!' and hugged us and the last thing we saw was Uncle Ernie's stick waving and his hair standing straight up on his head.

It was getting dark by this time and the buildings were like shadows and the lights in them seemed to be standing up alone in the air. We got the Mormon safely through New York though many people put their hands to their ears as we passed. Soon we were on the Parkway and the trees were marching beside us like tall dark friends. We felt sleepy and calm and the rattle of the Mormon shut us all in together and nobody said anything because it was not necessary.

At last we turned into the dirt road and saw the little white board with George W. Seaton on it. The house was blazing with lights and there on the porch was the whole family and they put their hands over their ears as we drove up.

'At last!' said Aunt Harriet. 'I thought something had happened.'

'O no,' said Pel, 'our angels took care of us.'

'Nonsense,' said Aunt Harriet, 'that Marmon would be too much for any angel.'

But Pel only laughed and said it had been a magical day and dropped her purse which Washington picked up. Then she got into the Mormon and moved all the handles and the rattle began.

And suddenly everybody began to laugh. The kind of laughter that comes all at once out of the middle of you and you cannot tell why. It just runs out of you like a fountain and you feel all light and empty. We laughed and waved to Pel and she laughed and waved back and the Mormon rattled away down the drive.

'Oh, *dear*.' said Aunt Harriet. 'What *are* we laughing at? Come in to supper.' But James said 'O, just let us listen till the veriest last moment!'

So we all stood on the porch listening till the car was safely down the hill. Then it hummed and rattled on to the Parkway and grew fainter and fainter and we heard it no more.

Aunt Harriet said very softly as if she did not want to break a spell, 'Shall we go in?' So we all went in an arm-in-arm procession and at the door of the dining-room James said to me 'Let us never forget today, shall we never?'

And I agreed that we would not.

... *September*

Today's plan was a very good one. Aunt Harriet made most of it, of course, but the last part was God's. Micky and Patrick and James and I spent the morning picking corn and pumpkins and squashes for the Harvest Festival, and Aunt Harriet walked up and down like a sentry telling us which ones to pick. Every now and then she would point her stick and say 'Pick that one, James. It will make a nice Pie.' Or 'don't pick that way, Sabrina, it takes too much energy. Give it a Short Sharp Twist.'

You could see that this was a very important day for her because the fruits of the earth had ripened. After a time my hand got tired of giving Short Sharp Twists so I just walked up and down with Aunt Harriet sharing her proud glances at the pumpkins. And presently she said in a whisper 'Lets you and me go and have some grapes.' So we went into the arbour and held the big blue bunches in our hands and nuzzled them like ponies. 'They're not really ripe yet,' said Aunt Harriet 'but aren't they *good!*' And she looked guilty and delighted just like a little girl. Then suddenly she looked at her watch and said 'Micky! Just run over to the Mayday's and ask how things are going.' And presently Micky came back and said 'No change. The divil a change in it at all. But going well.'

'What's going well?' said James but Aunt Harriet said he couldn't do two things at once. 'Either ask questions or pick,' she said 'and it would be more helpful, James, if you would pick?'

Then it was luncheon and after that we put on our best clothes to look nice for Washington because we were going to his School to see him play Baseball. This was our first Baseball Match. When we drove up to the school there were banners flying everywhere and from the top of the pavilion the American flag. This is called Old Glory which I think is a lovely name for it.

Many people came up and greeted Aunt Harriet and said they were expecting Washington to do his best pitching. When we were pushing our way along the grand stand I heard some of them whispering that Mrs Seaton had brought her little Refugees with her. We do not mind being called that any more because they know now we are not Poles or Belgians in soup kitchens.

The sun shone over us like a big umbrella and in front of us was a large green field with four things that looked like flour-bags dotted round it in a semicircle. 'Those are the Bases.' said Aunt Harriet, whispering as though she were in church.

Presently nine large boys in blue tops and red bottoms came out and after them nine more with white tops and green bottoms and we all cheered. Then the white and greens (which I shall now call just Greens) went out to field and one of the blue and reds (now called Reds) stood by one of the bags with a long thin Indian Club in his hands looking fierce and shy at the same time. Then one of the Greens took a ball from another and looked at it furiously. Next he turned round and began to wave his arm and clap the ball in his two hands and jerk his knee up so that it nearly hit his stomach. He made the most terrible faces all the time he was doing this and the crowd cheered and the ball flew out of his hand and the Red hit it with the Indian Club and the terrible-faced boy caught it again. Aunt Harriet shouted 'Bravo, Washington!' and shook her umbrella. And would you believe it, the man making all those faces and getting in such a knot was Washington! So James and I shouted too.

Then the first Red ran to the first bag and another came in and Washington did the same awful things to him and so on for several Reds. And James said 'I hope he won't kill anybody.' And Aunt Harriet replied 'Why, James, Washington wouldn't hurt a fly.' At that moment Washington handed the ball to another Green and the Reds ran from bag to bag and everybody shouted. Baseball is a kind of Rounders only you make more faces while you play it and have a round bat instead of a flat one. It is a bit like Cricket, too, so Burton need not have called James a Sissy.

Then suddenly everybody stood up except James who was reading his programme and did not notice. And Aunt Harriet said quite sternly for her 'Stand up, please, James!' And he jumped up and said 'Are we going to sing a hymn!' 'Certainly not!' she said 'This is the end of the Seventh innings and we always stand up for that.'

'O, just like God Save the King.' said James.

After that there were some more innings for each side and Aunt Harriet got horser and horser shouting 'Bravo!' And when it was over everybody waved umbrellas and bags and handkerchiefs and cheered.

'Who has won?' said James. But Aunt Harriet had lost her voice and could only wave her umbrella.

'Nod or shake your head' said James. 'Blue and Red?' Aunt Harriet shook her head. 'White and green?' She nodded so we knew that Washington's side had won.

Then the crowd began to move all except one elderly lady who sat there and let everybody go past her. When we got up to her we discovered it was Aunt Porter. She said 'He's my godson, so I felt it was up to me to come. But I do wish, Harriet, that Washington could have been a Stargazer. So much less strenuos for everybody.' Then she got up and sauntered away.

As we drove home Washington sat in the front seat looking very pleased and dirty and Aunt Harriet sat in the back looking very pleased and clean and saying over and over again in a sort of starling's squawk 'Bravo Washington!' and when Uncle George heard the news he gave him a ten-dollar bill.

That was the end of Aunt Harriet's part of the day. Her voice was quite gone and she was just going upstairs to gargle when the front door opened and Mr Mayday came in looking extra large with a big cigar in his mouth.

'Well, how is she?' hissed Aunt Harriet. And he grew larger still and said 'Very well. All over. A boy.'

That was God's part of the plan. The baby had been born at two o'clock this afternoon and Mr Mayday had come over to tell the news and to say that Mrs Mayday would like James and me to go over and see her.

So Aunt Harriet hugged Mr Mayday and croaked Hooray and said of course we could go.

The house was all hung with sheets and smelt like the

hospital where James had his tonsils out. Mrs Mayday's voice said 'Come in, S-a-b-r-i-n-a D-e-a-r' and Mr Mayday gave us a little push through the door. She was in bed looking quite well and pretty and beside the bed was a very small cot. You could just see the top of the baby's head covered with dark fur.

James said 'Well, it has dived out. Did it hurt? Cows hurt quite a lot. I know because I have helped Jim Leeves.' She said 'Well, it did. Quite a bit.' But she did not look as if she minded now.

'Wasn't he clever,' said James, 'to know just the right moment to dive?' And Mrs Mayday said 'O, he's terribly clever. The most gifted boy. Don't you want to see him, S-a-b-r-i-n-a?' I nodded and my tongue felt rather tickly and the nurse picked the baby out of its cot and held it for us to see. 'Look!' said Mr Mayday, 'Finger nails! And a nose! And quite a bit of hair!' And the baby's hands stretched and curled like starfish and his mouth buttoned and unbuttoned greedily.

'Let S-a-b-r-i-n-a hold him.' said Mrs Mayday and the nurse put him in my arms. I could feel his head inside one elbow and his feet inside another and his body pressed against my chest and it gave me a funny aching feeling inside. Then the nurse said 'That's enough now,' and Mrs Mayday said 'C-o-m-e t-o-m-o-r-r-o-w' and Mr Mayday brought us home through the wood.

'This is an occasion, Charles,' Uncle George said when we got in.

And he opened a fat bottle with a loud pop and gave James and me a small glass between us while they finished the bottle. So we drank the baby's health and the wine tasted like bitter lemonade and presently James said 'I feel rather sizzly in my head.' So Uncle George sent us to bed and we tiptoed past Aunt Harriet's room so as not to wake her.

James has just called out to me in a queer voice 'I say, Sabrina, I seem to be doing something silly. What is it?' And I went in and found him trying to put his pyjamas on over his clothes. So I helped him to undress and he fell asleep before he was even in bed.

But my head is not sizzling and I can write in my dairy. I am thinking about the baby and that James and I must have been as small as that once, and fitted into Mother's elbow just as nicely. She must have had that same clear new look Mrs Mayday had tonight and someday I will have it too. I would like to feel the inside of my elbows filled up. But at the same time I feel rather small for all I will have to do. Perhaps it will be better when we are grown up and our bodies do not seem to be bursting with all the things we feel. Sometimes I feel I must have somebody to help me. I cannot do it all by myself. Goodnight.

*

Oh, dear, this has been a very exciting day. I must write it down in my dairy before I go to sleep or I shall forget. Today Aunt Harriet said we must rest and be quiet as she had a Special Plan for tonight. 'To sleep in the shrubbery?' said James looking wildly at her and she said 'No, a Surprise.' Which was a relief.

So we went into the wood and looked for some American nature and found a Salamander under a log. It is black with yellow spots rather like a lizard but even more like a leopard. Salamanders can live in the fire without burning up, Micky says. They are like the Banshee and never die but are Immortal. But when we wanted to make a fire and try it he said 'Faith then, you'll not for fear the tales would be groundless.' So we put it in the cigarette tin with the green catterpillar which is now dead and are keeping it for Mrs Mayday's baby when he is old enough to Appreciate it. We were just catching a few flies to feed it when Aunt Harriet's voice called anxiously from the house. When we got to her she said 'In two minutes the King is going to speak. Do you want to hear him?'

There were several friends of Aunt Harriet in the drawing-room and the radio was saying 'In just one minute we shall take you over to London, England. One minute, please.' Then there were cracklings and poppings and rush-ing roaring sounds and the Atlantic Ocean seemed to be

rolling to us through the radio. Somebody said 'Sit down, children.' But James said No and suddenly everybody else got out of their chairs and stood up too.

Then we heard his voice. It came very carefully and strongly over the waters and seemed to hit us in our stomachs. I thought the whole world must be listening. Mother would be standing by the drawing-room hearth at Thornfield and Father would be listening somewhere else in the R.A.F. and they would know that we would be listening too. I felt that all four of us were together again and that London was just round the corner with Big Ben striking and Buckingham Palace and St Paul's and the Green Park with the Ducks and Pimlico where Miss Minnett's sister lives and Bean's Hotel and the Thames.

When he had finished speaking there came the roll of drums that always makes you feel a little sick and then God Save the King which is not a very good tune as music, Father says, but all the same it always makes you rumble. It was still rumbling inside me when Aunt Harriet sent us away to get ready for lunch.

We spent a very profitable afternoon fishing in the pond for water-midges to feed the salamander and then we went to the kitchen to talk to Nelly and Katie and they were putting cups and knives and plates and Coke bottles into a large clothes basket. 'What's that for?' said James and Katie said they were for the Picnic tonight so we knew that that was the Surprise. But we did not tell Aunt Harriet we knew so that she could have the pleasure of surprising us and we could have the pleasure of Anticipation. It works both ways.

When it was dark Georgina and Washington arrived with two boys, McAlister and Robert who are some of the Beaux out of Georgina's box and two girls called Barbara and Caroline-Ann. Then Uncle George appeared all hung about with rugs and coats and mackintoshes and Aunt Harriet with a long fishnet wound round and round her head against the midges.

'Pile in!' said Uncle George and we got into the station waggon and went bumping round the back drive and through the woods and over the fields with the headlights making a road of light in the darkness. There we found Micky and Pat standing up like ghoshts behind the flames of a huge fire and everybody began shouting different orders and banging crockery and arguing and altering the fire. 'Wait!' said Aunt Harriet just as Uncle George was shaking cocktails and pouring them out 'We must wait for Charlotte!' Before we could wonder who Charlotte was Washington called out 'Here she comes!' And down the field came a very old-fashioned car rumbling and squeaking. A little man in overalls and yellow gloves and a sea-going cap jumped out and opened the door and out came several shawls and rugs and inside them was a very tall and wide old lady with an Alsatian dog on a lead.

Everybody called out 'Welcome!' and she tossed off the shawls and came slowly over the grass, very steady and secure like a ship coming alongside a wharf. Then it turned out that she was Caroline-Ann's grandmother and a great freind of Aunt Harriet's and her name is Mrs Floriano. The little man and Uncle George made a throne of rugs for her and she sat down on it like a queen and said 'Thank you, George. Thank you, Piet!' And you felt it was not just manners but that she really was thanking them. The little man sat down behind her like a bodyguard and held the dog.

After this Diversion everybody began shouting and demanding drinks and if you were young you had Coke and if old Cocktails. Then Washington and Micky fried Hamburgers and sausages and everybody ate and ate very hungrily because of the night air. James passed the salt and pepper many times to Barbara and Caroline-Ann even when they already had it which was rather fussy of him. We kept on eating and eating and our legs got very hot and our backs got very cold and the flames flickered over all the faces and made them dance.

'Have you brought your Giutar, Piet?' said Uncle George and Mrs Floriano sent the little man to get his Giutar from the car.

'You know,' she said to James and me 'he is a very special sort of person. There is nothing he cannot do. He was born in Venice and when he was young he used to dig marble out of the Carrara mountains. I dare say Piet is responsible for most of the modern statues in the world. He has been a soldier and a cook and a waiter and a tightrope walker. He is very good with babies, too, and an excellent carpenter. Once he was wrecked on a desert island and after that he became a bird-fancier and now he stokes my furnace.'

Piet seemed a very small man to have so much Past in him. He smiled and looked at us shyly like a little woodland animal and then he began to tune up his giutar behind Mrs Floriano. She sat very still watching everything calmly and not talking much. You could feel that she had a lot of life behind her, too, and that it had made her steady and endless and undeniable like History. Even to die would not surprise her, it would be just pulling slowly in to another wharf.

Then Piet began to play and we all lay back on our rugs and listened to him. The trees stood round in a dark ring and the lake was very black except where the fire touched it. The night seemed to come down over us and the stars closer and we could see the Little Bear which is called the Dipper in the United States and Cassieopeia and Aldebaran the Wanderer and Cor Hydrae, the Lonely One, the same stars that Father taught us, all keeping watch over America and England.

'No, James!' said Aunt Harriet suddenly as he was reaching for another Coke. 'You've had five already!' But Uncle

George said lazily, 'Let him have it. This is the land of Liberty.'

So James had another. 'I wish I could see Liberty,' he said.

'You can't *see* liberty, Silly,' said Georgina. 'It's an Abstract Noun.'

'You can so, too.' said James. 'Standing up in the water just near New York. I've seen pictures.'

'He means the Statue' said Aunt Harriet.

'Of course he does!' said Mrs Floriano. 'And he shall see it. Piet used to be one of the men who looked after Liberty's rivets. He can take them.'

When she said that Piet smiled at us and James said he would give Mrs Floriano his new flashlight and she thanked calmly and said she would be glad of it.

Then Piet twanged his guitar again and Uncle George began to hum out of tune, keeping time by waving the hand with the cocktail shaker in it. And one after another we joined in till we were all singing. We sang,

> 'Drink to me only with thine eyes
> And I will pledge with mine,
> Or leave a kiss within the cup
> And I'll not ask for wine,
> The thirst that from the soul doth rise
> Doth ask a gift divine

But might I of Jove's nectar sup
I would not change for thine.'

And then,

'Oh, I went down South for to see my Sal,
   Sing Polly Wolly Doodle all the Day,
My Sal she am a saucy Gal,
   Sing Polly Wolly Doodle all the Day,
     Fare thee well, Fare thee well,
     Fare thee well, my faery fay,
     For I'm off to Louisianna
     For to see my Susyanna
   Sing Polly Wolly Doodle all the Day'

And,

'The Animals went in Two by Too,
   There's one more river to cross,
The elephant and the kangaroo,
   There's one more river to cross.
One More River, and that's the river of Jordan
One More River, there's one more river to cross.'

Then Uncle George said 'Now, you two! Give us something from over the water.' So James and I sang together

'I know where I'm going
   And I know who's going with me,
I know who I love
   But the dear knows who I'll marry.'

After the first verse Piet picked up the music on his guitar.

'I have stockings of silk
   Shoes of fine green leather,
Combs to buckle my hair
   And a ring for every finger.

Some say he's black
   But I say he's bonny
The fairest of them all
   My handsome, winsome Johnny.

Feather beds are soft
   And painted rooms are bonny
But I would leave them all
   To go with my love Johnny.

I know where I'm going
   And I know who's going with me,
I know who I love
   But the dear knows who I'll marry.'

When we had finished everybody was silent and the fire and the stars crackled in the darkness and Aunt Harriet put her arms round us and the fishnet tickled our noses. Piet said 'Bella. Molta Bella.' That is Italian. That was the first time he had spoken and his voice was just like a very small animal's.

Then Aunt Harriet looked at her watch and said 'Glory Sakes! It's ten o'clock. You children should be in bed. Pack up, pack up!'

It is not nearly so much fun packing after a picnic as it is before. Everybody argued where everything should go and a great search had to be made for the frying-pan because it is Katie's treasure. Micky poured water over the fire and I stamped on the embers till they were black and James guided Mrs Floriano to her car and left his flashlight with her and came away quickly in case he should repent. There was nothing left but starlight to guide us until we got into the car and the lamps made a bright lane through the woods. The plates and cups rattled behind us and we all talked drowsily the way you do when you are nearly asleep and have eaten a good deal.

But we woke up when the car stopped and we are in bed now, talking through the door while I write in my dairy. James has just said 'Fancy a Salamander being able to live in the fire!'

And I said Yes.

Then he said 'Piet is like a very small animal, isn't he?'
And I said Yes.
He said 'Could you hear the Atlantic in the radio today?'
And I said Yes.
He said 'Do you think They were listening too?'
And I said Yes.

... *September*

This morning Mrs Floriano rang up and I answered the telephone. And she said 'Tell Aunt Harriet that if she hasn't made a plan for today I've got one.' Then Aunt Harriet came and discussed it with Mrs Floriano and when she had finished she said 'Hurry up, Sabrina and James! Get hats and coats and be ready to go off with Uncle George.'

Uncle George always rushes his breakfast and he hustled us so much that I had to leave half my bacon. The next thing we knew we were in the train with him and James was asking where we were going. Uncle George looked round the corner of his paper and just said 'You'll see, fella.' and dived behind it again. No man likes being talked to or asked questions early in the morning. Father says Noon is time enough for family life to begin. So we just looked out of the window and watched the cemeteries and stations till we came to New York. One of the stations is called Valhalla which is the place where the gods go when they are dead, if gods can die, but you would never think it would look like this.

When we got to New York Uncle George hustled us into a taxi and said 'Battery!' and soon we were riding through the canyons between the buildings and New York looked just as sunny as it did on the day with Pel. Presently the canyons stopped at the very edge of the sea and we dashed out of the taxi and ran towards it because it was so long since we'd seen it. 'Hi, this way!' called Uncle George walking across a little park to a round white house. There was a small figure waiting beside the little house and it came towards us and smiled shyly and said 'Buon Giorno.' (Italian for Good Day.) It was Piet, so of course we knew then where we were going. This time he did not have overalls but a checked coat but the yellow gloves and the sea-going cap were just the same.

'Take care of them, Piet.' said Uncle George and went back to the taxi and Piet and James and I sat on a rail watching the sea and the gulls and the ferryboats. Across the water stood the Statue of Liberty holding up her hand as if she were saying 'Hi!' or perhaps 'Stop!' 'Why does she have a crown of thorns?' said James but Piet said they were not thorns but only spikes. A big ferry boat was coming slowly and steadily towards us just like Mrs Floriano. We asked Piet how she was and he said 'Fine. She greata bigga da queen. Bellissima.' And he kissed his fingers to the air. Then he said quickly 'You likea da Hokey-pokey?' and ran to a little cart on the quay and came back with two large cones of Ice Cream. This is what Hokey-Pokey means. By the time we had finished the cones the ferry-boat had arrived and we all went up to the top deck. The ship grumbled and started again and we sat in the wind watching everything. Piet showed us where Staten Island was and Brooklyn and the Hudson and East Rivers and gradually we drew nearer the Statue of Liberty which Americans are very proud of because it made them free like Magna Carta.

On the way James asked Piet if he minded going about with English people.

'You tella me for why I mind, hey?' said Piet in his gentle voice.

'Well, because England and Italy are fighting each other just now,' explained James.

'So what?' said Piet. 'Why for I get in a tear? I no more Italiano. Saluta da American flag now. Also, why we makea *more* fight, you and me? Hey? You wanta war? No. I wanta war? No. Who pay for da war, da bigga stupida fella shoota da mouth off? No. *We* pay. You and me. All mens likea da peace, live in da sun, drinka da vino, playa guitar. Why we makea da war like bad boys, hey? We gotta Live gooda life like chucks in da wood. Yes?'

It was funny he should say that when he is just like a

woodchuck himself. Piet is too grown up to be warful and angry. He likes to sit in the sun and drink wine.

All this time the ferry boat was cutting through the blue water and presently we got off at a little pier and smelt seaweed and walked on to the little island where Liberty stands. We were very surprised to find how large she was. From the shore she looks small and friendly and not large enough for anybody to get inside her. But from her own island she seems enormous and she has rather a fierce occupied look as though she were so busy keeping America free that she had no time for anything else. It makes you ache to watch her arm stretched out like that all the time. You feel it must get tired.

The first thing we did was to buy a post card telling us the size of all the different features and then we took an elevator as far as the top of the pedestal because the Statue does not begin till you are there. After that you begin to climb a circular staircase and presently you are really inside Liberty. Outside she is all green but inside she is all beige and everywhere there are rivets which hold her together, the very ones Piet used to look after in his Younger Days. We followed the snaky staircase round and round and felt her skirts flowing down over us as we climbed.

'Look,' said James, 'There is her foot.'

And Piet said 'O, da leetle foot. Piccola.' and laughed.

It was a very large foot. If we had allowed him James

would have leaned over the staircase and put his head into it. His hand would have fitted easily into the smallest toe.

Round and round we went getting rather dizzy and trying all the time to guess what part of her outside we were inside. The folds of her nightgown spreading down to her feet went on for a long time. And all the way inside Liberty's skin and on the staircase there were names scribbled and initials inside hearts and remarks. Presently Piet said 'Now we are inside da greata bigga da chest' and he swelled out his cheeks so that we could see how really big it was. 'Looka, looka!' he said and pointed and there printed in large letters in a very dangerous place were the words PIETRO ANFOSSI. Piet laughed and said 'Thata me! I writea my name on the vera tippa da chest. Pretty good, hey, pretty funny!' And he began rolling round with laughter, and waving at his name in a very friendly way. I suppose he put it there one day when he was testing the rivets.

Then we left the chest and went on round and round through Liberty's face. Her mouth is three feet wide, think of that, and her nose is four feet six inches long and there is a great hole inside where it sticks out outside. The post card does not say how large her eyes are but there are two feet and six inches between them. At last we came to an open space and Piet said 'Toppa da head. Now we look out through the crown!' Forty people can stand inside Liberty's head but today there were only Piet and James and I. There

was a row of little windows all round under the spikes of the crown and we looked out. Far away we could see the harbour joining the sea and on the other side the flamy buildings of New York standing up in the sun and down below little ships moving along the water. And while we looked we could feel Liberty swinging gently with us inside her. It would be dreadful if she ever fell off the pedestal. What would America do?

At last we had looked at everything so we came down another staircase noticing her back this time instead of her front. But we passed the foot again at the bottom before we got into the lift.

Then we were outside and Liberty was swaying dangerously above us and gazing out to sea.

On the little pier James suddenly stopped and jumped down to get shells from the shore. But Piet dived after him and said 'Bambino, you stay closea da me. Great bigga rats down there. Bigga da cats. I tella you.' Which was disappointing as we would both like to have seen rats as big as cats.

There was a little shop on the ship called NOVELTIES so we bought presents for everybody and they all had the Statue of Liberty on them. Aunt Harriet's was a cushion cover and it had New York as well and a Red Rose and Two Love Birds. Also this verse,

'Sweetheart, I thought that you would like to know
That someone's thoughts go where you go,
That someone never can forget
The hours we spent since first we met,
That life is richer, sweeter far
For such a sweetheart as you are
And now my constant prayer will be
That God will keep you safe for me.'

When the ship docked we looked back at Liberty and she had grown down again to her normal size. Then we went to an Italian restuarant with Piet and wound spaghetti round our forks and drank Coke. And while we ate Piet talked ardent Italian to the waiter whose name is Teo and he used to help Piet rivet Liberty. After that there was another taxi that stopped outside a gorgeous tall building that looked like the Arabian nights. Inside was a big marble hall just like a cathedral and several men were walking about silently and reverently. 'Why are we in church?' said James 'It isn't Sunday.' But Piet shook his head and whispered solemnly 'Dis placea da Beeg Business.' And presently we heard Uncle George's voice saying 'Well, here you are!' quite loudly and it turned out that these marble halls were his office. You wouldn't think how he could dare do business in them but he does not seem to think them too splendid.

So then we all went back together in the train and Piet

drove away in Mrs Floriano's old-fashioned car waving the red handkerchief with the Statue of Liberty on it that we had given him. And when we got home everybody was very pleased to see us and asked us about everything just as though we had been on a long journey. They were delighted with their presents and it turned out that the cushion was just what Aunt Harriet had always wanted especially the verse part which she said was a Great Tribute and very comforting.

'And now,' said James, 'I think we'd better go quietly and not have too many surprises for a bit or you will run out of them.'

'Well, I don't see why.' said Aunt Harriet, 'You've hardly touched the fringe yet. Still, perhaps it is a good thing to have something up your sleeve.'

'Have you something up your sleeve?' said James.

'Well, yes,' said Aunt Harriet. 'Can you guess it?'

But we couldn't. Her face crinkled up then with its secret and she laughed and said 'You are going to school on Monday.'

'Glory sakes!' said James. 'Why didn't you tell us before?'

'Why, James, don't you want to go to school?' she said.

And he said 'Y-e-s. But I would like to have more time to get used to the idea. Of course I want to go. Of course. Of course.' And each time he said Of Course he said it more loudly.

But when we came upstairs to bed he looked wildly at me and said 'What will it be like? Hundreds of people, do you think? All talking at once in a big buzz? Making you lose little bits of yourself every minute?'

But how can I say? I don't know any more than he does. When you are only used to small schools and Miss Minnett and Mr Oliphant the thought of a big one in a strange country makes you anxious. Perhaps we will be Ignoramuses. I can hear James in his room saying his Multiplications and spelling out words. He is rather worried. And so am I. Now the difficult part of America begins.

But we will do it. We can take it. It will be O.K. Goodnight.

... September

This has been our first day at the Lime Ridge School and so much has happened that I cannot squeeze it all into words. Besides, I am too tired. Lime Ridge is not a bit like a school to look at. It is a large white house with arcades and pillars and a fountain in the courtyard and a large red barn which is a gymnasium inside. The Headmaster is Mr Sherstone who lookes like Father Christmas without his beard and he pushes through the crowds of children like a horse scattering a pack of hounds. Except in the Lord Mayor's Procession I never saw so many people all at once. There must be hundreds.

Well, the day began with Assembly which is where you assemble and have a prayer and a hymn with Mr Sherstone and he says a few words about the New Term. After that I was marched away to Grade Seven because that is the grade for my age and James was marched away to Grade Five because he is the age for that. He looked at me with his wild drowning look as he went but I could not do anything about it because of course we cannot do everything together any more. But I wanted to run after him, all the same and tell him it would be all right.

Two girls called Fortune and Meta took charge of me and showed me where to go. Fortune has red hair and freckles and glasses and Meta has black hair and a beautiful pink face and blue eyes. Fortune's face is kinder, though, because it really looks at you. Meta is going to be a Movie Star when she grows up. Well, the first lesson we had was Social Studies which is the American word for plain History. We had it with a man called Mr Smith and it was all about America. When we do History at home America seems a very small spot in the corner of your mind. But here it is the other way round and England is the very small spot. Mr Smith is very nice and his name gave me a beautiful homely feeling. When the lesson was over he asked me about all I had learnt and I told him about Miss Minnett and Mr Oliphant. He says my grade doesn't do Algebra or Geometry or Shakespeare yet or English

Literature but that it is much further on than I am in Mathematics so that some of it will be hard and some of it will be easy. Then he told me he had an aunt in Surrey and that he was very fond of England having been there on a walking tour. After that he told Fortune to take me to dinner.

James was not at my table but he ran up to me on the way to his and said 'Sabrina, what do you think? I have to *rest* after lunch. All my Grade does it. Must I? I'm not a bit tired.' But before I could answer he was whisked away. In school you have no Peace.

At Lime Ridge you do not get marks but A.B.C.D. Fortune said you had to be a moron to get E. A Moron is an idiot. 'I often get E.' said Meta and Fortune said 'Well, there you are!' But Meta did not mind because she said there was more to life than just getting educated. If you get a lot of A's during one term you get on the Roll of Honour but you are quite liable to fall off it the next if you do not work hard.

This afternoon we had French which was very easy because it was only a few verbs and nouns and you could speak in English during the lesson which is impossible with Miss Minnett because she makes you ask everything in French and if you slip up too many times she calls Mother in. After that it is French day in and day out until you improve. French was with Mr Smith. His accent is not so good as Miss Minnett's but it is more interesting and his teeth do not clatter up and down.

The last lesson of all was singing which we did in the Barn with a tall lady with two very large ear-rings. Her name is Mrs Mott and she kept stopping us and saying 'No, no. I want *human* sounds. Not the bleat of a rabbit. Now, ah, ah, ah, ah, ah!' James's grade had the lesson with ours and in the middle of 'Believe me if all' I noticed Mrs Mott open her eyes wide and look at James. At the end of the song she asked him his name and made him come out in front of the whole class. I did not dare to look at him but I knew what he was feeling. 'Let me hear you sing the scale' she said. And when he sang it very clearly she said 'Now, the song!' And he sang,

> 'Believe me if all those endearing young charms
> Which I gaze on so fondly today
> Were to change by tomorrow and fleet in my arms
> Like fairy gifts fading away,
> Thou would'st still be adored as this moment thou art
> Let thy loveliness fade as it will
> And around the dear ruin each wish of my heart
> Would entwine itself verdantly still.'

I could not help loving him, he seemed such a little boy to be singing about ruins.

Then Mrs Mott said 'Now, that is how I want *everybody* to sing!' and James went red with shame and hurried back to his seat and hid his head behind a larger boy.

Then suddenly school was over for the day and we were running to meet Micky. Georgina flung herself into the car and said 'Well, how did you get on?' 'Oh, it was easy! I could do everything easily!' said James. And by that I knew that he had found it rather hard. Then he said in a much smaller voice 'My spelling is Frightful.' 'Pooh,' said Georgina, 'so is mine. That's nothing,' But I don't believe it is really because she was on the Roll of Honour last term. She was only saying it to keep James' Countenance.

Everybody wanted to know all about school when we got home and Aunt Harriet sent us to bed early because she said the first day was always the worst and exhausting. So now we are in bed and I am remembering all I can. If I were at home I would remember it out loud to Mother and feel all the scattered bits of myself being gathered together in the evening. I would tell her about James singing and Fortune and Mr Smith's aunt. She is very good at listening and you feel yourself growing in her as though you were a tree. I hope they will not drop bombs on Mr Smith's aunt. Surrey is very near London.

*

. . . September

Life is so busy now that I cannot always keep up with my dairy. Gradually we are getting used to school but it takes up a lot of precious time. Also we have a great many friends who can come to tea or supper whenever we like. It is wonderful the amount of noise Aunt Harriet can bear. But Uncle George says he often wishes he could live in a Padded Cell.

Of course, School isn't easy all the time. I often get into trouble though nobody has reported me to Mr Sherstone yet. The worse thing is Staring out of the Window. Mr Smith says that it is not so bad looking out of the window if you are looking at *something* but that looking at nothing is just day-dreaming and not a thing to be encouraged. I do not know how to explain to him that I always *am* looking at something but it is not always outside. Sometimes it is inside my head.

Also, although most of the lessons are easier than they are in England I am still rather bad at Maths. Whenever I have to paper a room I always put it on the ceiling, too, or else paper the room solid. Mr Smith is often disappointed in me.

James is good at everything except spelling and Arts and Crafts. He can do anything with his mind but his hands are not so clever.

Now I must do my homework. Goodnight.

. . . October
School.

. . . October
Fortune had toothache so she could not come to tea.

. . . October
School. All my sums were right today and Aunt Harriet said
Halleluyah and Uncle George gave me a dollar.

. . . October
School. And Fortune came to supper tonight. She is still my
Favourite Friend. She is very worried just now and thinks
she will die young because of her frightful Toothache. It is
a funny thing but until lately I have never thought of dying.
When you are young you think you will go on forever.
Then one day you realise that you won't and it is terrible.
Fortune has known for a long time that she would die someday but I have only just realised. On the other hand, I have
always known about babies and she has only just discovered
and thinks it is Awful.

Today there was the Incident of Alexander. He is an English boy who has just come to Lime Ridge and speaks in one of those voices that are silly even in England but much more silly in America. You know, a pernicketty voice. He is in a grade below me and a grade higher than James and has black hair and a fat face. Well, today Alexander got very uppish and said that America was Absolutely Filthy so I said Why? 'Well, to begin with,' he said 'they don't know anything about lessons. Here I am not doing any Latin at all.' I said 'Well, that's a good thing, you don't have to go around saying Quis and Ego and showing everybody how clever you are. Besides, it saves a lot of trouble.' He said 'No, it doesn't. I have to think of my Career. My Father's a Civil Servant.' I said 'My Father's a servant of the King. He's in the R.A.F.' He said 'It's worse for me. I was going to Westminster.'

'Pooh,' said James, 'Jason Campbell was going to Eton and he doesn't mind. He likes going to school in America.' 'Pooh, what's America?' said Alexander. 'A potty little country at the end of nowhere.' So James got very white and said 'If you think its so potty, put your hands up!' Alexander just laughed but he laughed too soon because James let out his fist and socked him and Alexander said 'Ow!' and hit James with his flat hand. James said 'Come on, fight!' And he danced round Alexander and socked him another and Alexander hit him with a flat hand again. 'Say it, go on, say it!' said James, dancing with his teeth clinched. 'Is it potty?' And suddenly Alexander got quite white except where there were red marks on his chin and he said 'No, it isn't. I'm not saying that because I'm afraid, because I'm not. But it isn't potty.' Then he pushed through the crowd and walked away looking lonely and proud.

James was quite right to fight him but I could not bear to see Alexander like that so when nobody was noticing I ran after him and walked beside him. At first he wouldn't take any notice of me but when we got to the end of the field I said 'I expect you're homesick.' And he said 'I expect I am.' I said 'It gets better after a while. Will you come to tea tomorrow.' And he said 'Yes, I will.'

When I told James tonight he said 'Oh, good.' He had quite forgotten about fighting Alexander this morning.

... October

Winter came today. When we woke up there was a thick white frost on the ground and I could hear Uncle George roaring through the hall downstairs 'Georgy, James, Sabrina!' and when we got down he said 'If you want to see a wonderful sight, come on!' So we all stood on the running board of the car and instead of driving out of the gate Uncle George turned off and drove straight across the fields to the place where the river flows in a big waterfall down through the woods to the lake. We got out and walked with him through the woods. It was icy cold in spite of the sun and suddenly James said, cocking his head, 'Listen, the waterfall's stopped!'

'See why!' said Uncle George and we hurried ahead of him and found that the waterfall was quite frozen and over it the ice had spread in a great folding shawl right down to the lake. It was so wonderful that we could say nothing but 'O!' but in the silence we heard a little thread of water trickling down behind the ice, the smallest whisper, like a secret.

Uncle George said 'That's the beginning of winter.' And Georgina said 'Whoopee, soon we'll be skating!' And she began slithering and sliding and slipping over the frost as though she were quite young again. Then James began sliding and shouting and Uncle George, too, and we all joined hands and danced in the wood, singing and shouting and stamping and scrunching by the still waterfall. Our foot marks were like the marks of woodland animals in the frost and everything was glistening in the sun.

'Run!' said Uncle George, 'or you'll be late for school.'

So we raced to the car and fell into it all out of breath with laughing and dancing and James said 'O, will it ever be as bright again?'

'Of course, Silly!' said Georgina.

'Sure! Brighter!' said Uncle George.

And suddenly the dancing feeling went out of me and I felt it was unlucky to talk like that and I could not say anything.

... October

This is the last time I shall write in my dairy. Sometimes things happen too quickly and it makes your heart ache to write them and you cannot face the words on the page. Today everything has come at once like the river in flood and now that I am in bed I must remember them carefully one by one. I must do it with my mind for if I think about them in my heart I cannot write.

Today is James' birthday. He is nine years old. A Birthday is always a great day in our family and so it is in Aunt Harriet's. When we got up the sun was streaming over the red and gold leaves of the wood and making the frost sparkle like sugar. And when we came down to breakfast there was everybody standing at their places and as soon as they saw James they began to sing

> 'Happy birthday to you,
> Happy birthday to you,
> Happy birthday dear Ja-ames,
> Happy birthday to you!'

And James got very red and shy and they all laughed and hugged him and said Many Happy Returns and then Uncle George led him cerimoniously to his place and there by his plate was a pile of packages all done up in coloured paper and silver string. James stood very still looking at them and not saying anything until at last Aunt Harriet said 'Well, aren't you going to open them?' 'I like to look at them as they are first,' he said. 'I like to guess.' So then he handled all the parcels to see if he could guess them that way and after that he unwrapped them very slowly undoing the knots in a very irritating manner but I could understand because it is what I do myself.

'Must you untie *every* knot?' said Georgina, excitedly.

'Yes I must.' he said. 'And save the string.'

And as each present came out James said 'O, *just* what I wanted! How did you guess?' And examined it thorughly before going on to the next. Out of the first parcel came a watch, a large one to go in the pocket. That was from Uncle George and next came a very nobbly one from Aunt Harriet which took a lot of opening. And what do you think, it was a Microscope!

'Now I can examine a Fly's Wing and a Human Hair' said James excitedly and Aunt Harriet was very pleased he was pleased.

Then he opened a long packet and rushed at Georgina and hugged her and inside the packet was an Air Rifle that will slug a rabbit at fifty yards, the Booklet says. After that he opened my parcel which was a Rubber-tyred Truck which he said was a very good one. And so it ought to be for thirty-five cents.

'Thank you all.' said James and began to wrap the presents in their papers again.

'Hi, wait a bit!' said Washington. 'You've got nothing from me yet. Don't you want to look under the table?' So James looked under the table and there was a large carboard box covered with holes and tied up with rope and a large label on it that said 'Beware. Fragile. Open with Care.'

There were noisy scrabbilings and little squeaks coming from the box as James pulled it out and he nearly drove us all Mad by undoing every knot in the string. But at last it came undone and he took off the lid and there was, what do you think? A fox-hound puppy, all brown and black and fat and bumbly prancing about in the box and licking James' hand and squeaking and yelping. James said 'O!' and picked him out of the box and hugged him and said 'O!' again. Then he went round and stood beside Washington's chair hugging the puppy and saying nothing. But Washington understood perfectly because he said 'Well, what will you call him, Bud?' And James suddenly found his voice and said 'Trumpet!' very loudly and they all laughed and Trumpet is his name. He is quite the best animal that has happened to us since we said good-bye to the Mongrel Dog and James said except for not being at Thornfield it was quite the best birthday morning he had ever had.

Then Aunt Harriet said 'Bacon and eggs! And after that we will go shopping in the village and then drive over and see Aunt Porter and in the afternoon Pel will be coming and the Birthday Tea so there is a diversion for every minute of the day.' Then suddenly she looked at Trumpet and said 'Glory Sakes, Washington, you should have trained him first. I can't have *that* happening on my best carpet!' Trumpet looked at her quite sadly as though he understood and was sorry but the next minute it happened again so James said 'Wait!' and ran to the kitchen and came back with a cloth wrapped round a piece of stick like a banner and wiped up the carpet.

'On second thoughts,' said Aunt Harriet, 'I think perhaps You Two had better spend the morning training Trumpet in the way he should go. Otherwise we shan't have a carpet to our names.'

So we went into the woods and spent a lovely morning teaching Trumpet manners and trying to train him to follow a scent because James said when we go back to England he can come with us and hunt with the Eridge pack. But oh, as I write that I remember that perhaps we will never hunt with the Eridge again, perhaps nothing will ever be the same again. But I must not think about it or I cannot write.

At luncheon there was everything in America that James

likes best. Turky with chestnut stuffing and cranberries and sweet corn on the cob and lima beans and Pumpkin Pie. Aunt Harriet had thought it out very sweetly and carefully and James had two helpings of everything.

'I hope you have left room for the Cake this afternoon' she said as he got slowly down from the table.

'Only a very little.' he said, so Aunt Harriet said he had better go and lie down and he was quite glad to.

All the afternoon Aunt Harriet and Georgina and I were busy in the dining-room getting the party ready. At first the idea had been to have a very large one with lots of people from school but each time Aunt Harriet suggested a new Person James grew more and more silent until at last she said, 'Glory Sakes, James, don't you want *anybody* to your party?' And he shook his head and said 'Only my Treasures – you and Uncle George and Georgy and Washington and Sabrina and Aunt Porter and Pel. That's all I want.' And Aunt Harriet's eyes crinkled up in an understanding way and she said 'You shall have just what you want!'

Well, we decorated the table and hung up great strings of paper roses and a bell left over from last Christmas and when everything seemed Absolutely Perfect Aunt Harriet sent Georgina and me out because there was a special thing she did not want even us to see.

After that it was time for James to get up and presently a

ring came at the door and there was Aunt Porter. She came in on her springy feet and wrinkled her face at James and said 'There! Many Happy Returns!' and put a long thin little parcel into his hand. While he was opening it Aunt Porter noticed Trumpet. 'My Goodness,' she said, 'That's a very young dog. Harriet is going to be anxious about her carpets!' and I said she had been already.

Then the paper was off and James gave a very loud squeak of excitement just like Trumpet's. 'It's a present of a telescope!' he shrieked. 'No,' said Aunt Porter 'It's a present of the Universe. You'll soon know more about stars than I do.' She tried to look as though she minded that but her face danced up into a wrinkly smile. 'I must try it,' said James and we both looked through it but it was too light to see anything and we could only set it to the proper distance so that at night it would be all ready for picking out the stars.

'Now, come along, everything's ready!' said Aunt Harriet, coming out on to the porch. 'We won't wait for Pel. She said she might be late and as she usually is, anyway, we might as well go in. James first!'

So we all went in a long procession into the dining-room where Katie and Nelly and Micky and Patrick were already waiting and looking expectant and there in the middle of the table was an enormous Birthday Cake with Nine candles all alight and 'JAMES, MANY HAPPY RETURNS FROM HIS AMERICAN FAMILY' written on it in green and pink icing. And at the head of the table was Uncle George's arm-chair all twined about with roses and ivy and daisies and black-eyed-susans and red leaves and berries. And by the plate a great sceptre of gladiolas.

'Oh,' said James 'how did you know? That is what we do at home. The Birthday Person sits in Father's chair. How *did* you know?'

'We didn't.' said Aunt Harriet, 'It was Pel's idea and the flowers are her present. Take your place on the throne.'

So James sat down very proudly and leaned back among the roses and Trumpet curled up on the floor beside him and went to sleep.

After that we had tea and Uncle George made a funny solenm speech of congratulation and Micky kept saying 'Here, here!' and Aunt Porter drank James' health in a cup of china tea.

'Wish!' said Aunt Harriet as he cut the cake and he wished and we all wished for him and cracked the crackers and put on the paper caps and everything was very noisy and happy and nobody even murmured when Trumpet sprinkled again on the carpet. Everybody had to pull a cracker with James for luck and he got very excited and shouty and Georgina shouted to him to stop shouting and Washington shouted to Georgina to stop shouting herself and Uncle George roared out that *everybody* must stop shouting.

And just at that moment the door opened and Pel came in.

It was dark and the light stood up behind her and her eyes were very deep and still and she was not smiling. James cried out excitedly 'Oh, Pel, Pel, look at my presents! I've got—' But suddenly he stopped dead and ran to her. And I knew by the way she put her arm round him and held him that something had happened. 'What is it?' he said 'What is it?' And then 'Is it Them? Is it Father and Mother?' She shook her head and said softly 'No, no. They are all right. They are safe and well.'

I knew then what it was. I got down and went to her. 'Is it Thornfield?' And she said 'Yes, Sabrina.' Then she drew us to the table and we all listened while she told us that Father had sent her a cable saying there had been a great air battle over Sussex and that towards the end of it Thornfield had been hit by a bomb and partly destroyed and that bombs had fallen on Bell Farm across the Lane. She said that Father had told her to tell us that Mother was safe because she had been staying with Aunt Christina when it happened. And that we were not to be anxious.

She went on gently talking and everybody listened and said nothing and James kept cutting great slices of plum cake and stuffing it into his mouth until Aunt Harriet said 'James, lamb, won't you be ill?' But he said 'I must eat. I can't bear it. I must eat.' Then suddenly he shook Pel's arm and shouted 'Bell Farm! What about William and Walter and Susie. *They* weren't at Aunt Christina's. Where are William and Walter and Susie, tell me, tell me!' And she said 'I don't know, James. I don't know where they are. But I hope they are safe.' Then he burst into tears and she took him on to her knee and rocked him and everybody except Aunt Porter went out and left us alone in the dining-room. I kept remembering the sound of bombs as we heard them before we left and feeling the earth running and running under the house and thinking that it must have been just like that only louder when the bomb struck Thornfield. And James' sobbing got mixed up in my stomach with the sound of bombs and I could not tell which was which. Pel rocked him gently and looked at me across his head with a long deep look and soon he was quiet.

Then Aunt Porter got up slowly and she seemed suddenly to be very old and as though too many things had happened in her life. And she sighed and said half to herself and half to Pel 'We must build Jerusalem in England's green and pleasant land.' Pel nodded and said 'Yes, that is the job for James and Sabrina.' 'No,' said Aunt Porter, 'for us all.' And she took her stick and went quietly out.

Then we were all alone together and we sat by the birthday cake, very close, so as to keep warm. Pel said 'Tell me about School.' So we told her all we could think of, Mr Smith and Fortune and Alexander and James singing. We

went on talking on top of each other, talking and talking so as not to be thinking or feeling. Then Nelly came in to light the lights and Pel said she thought it would be a good idea if we went up to bed and that she would tuck us in.

So we said goodnight to Aunt Harriet and Uncle George and they hugged us tightly and looked anxiously at us as grown-ups do when they long to give you something and can't because there is nothing to give. And Aunt Harriet said I could use her Bathroom and the French Fern Soap and the Bath Salts.

Pel came with me and when I was in the bath I asked her what I had been trying to ask all the time. I wanted to know how much of Thornfield was gone, if it was the house or perhaps just only the stables and outhouses and garden. But she said truthfully 'I don't know, dear love. I know no more than you do. But however much is gone we will build it again. After the war you and James and Romulus and I will go back to Thornfield and we will all rebuild it together.' She looked very stern sitting there on the edge of the bath as though she had a sword in her hand and were going out to meet the enemy.

Then she turned to me and said, 'We must take everything that comes to us, Sabrina. Good or bad. Refuse nothing. It's the only way to live. You'll never be given more than you can take. And if you take it proudly it will not break you.'

And she looked at me long and lovingly as though she were begging me to take it. And suddenly I felt that I could and I said 'Yes, Pel.' And then her eyes filled with tears and she wrapped the towel round me and we cried together. Then she rubbed me down very hard and put my dressing-gown on me and tied the cord with two jerks saying 'There and there! Now, into bed.'

She went off to find James then and I lay in bed feeling calm and empty as though I had no tears left and thinking of Thornfield and Father and Mother and the days when we were young. And why there have to be wars that kill people who have not done any harm and destroy houses that have stood for so many years. And I thought, 'Oh, do let them be safe because we cannot lose them or bear any more.' And after that I felt that they would be safe and that some day it will be all right and we will be together again. I was thinking that when Pel came in with James.

I do not know what she had said to him but he looked all soft and rosie and smaller than usual and his hair was wet and shiny. 'James thinks it would be nice if he slept with you,' said Pel, 'and I have decided to stay the night so I shall be sleeping next door.' Then she tumbled James in beside me and said 'Wait a minute!' We heard her running downstairs and presently she came back with a clothes basket in her arms and in the basket was Trumpet sound asleep. 'Now,' she said, 'we are all together.'

She put Trumpet down beside the bed but he did not wake, just snored babyishly. Then she bent over us and made a mark on our foreheads and she said 'My golden ones,' and kissed us and went away. When she had gone James reached over me and picked Trumpet out of the basket and took him into bed between us. They both lay there very quietly while I got out my Dairy and wrote the story of this day.

Presently James said 'Sing to me, Sabrina.' so I sang some humming songs while I was writing. And now I have nearly finished and I shall not write in my dairy any more but just take what comes and not try to remember it every night.

'Have you finished?' said James. And I said Nearly.

'Then stop humming and sing. Sing something that says everything.' he said sleepily.

So I will sing the only song I know that says everything and then I will put out the light.

> 'Now the day is over
> Night is drawing nigh
> Shadows of the evening
> Steal across the sky.
>
> Jesus, give the weary
> Calm and sweet repose

With thy tenderest blessing
May our eyelids close.

Grant to little children
Visions bright of thee,
Guard the sailors tossing
On the deep blue sea.

Through the long night-watches
May thine angels spread
Their white wings above me
Watching round my bed.

When the morning wakens
Then may I arise
Pure and fresh and sinless
In thy holy eyes.

Glory to the Father
Glory to the Son
And to thee, blessed Spirit,
While the ages run.'

James is asleep. Goodnight.